THE **SHERLOCK LUCY JAMES** MYSTERIES

GALAHAD'S CASTLE

THE SHERLOCK HOLMES AND LUCY JAMES MYSTERIES

The Last Moriarty
The Wilhelm Conspiracy
Remember, Remember
The Crown Jewel Mystery
The Jubilee Problem
Death at the Diogenes Club
The Return of the Ripper
Die Again, Mr. Holmes
Watson on the Orient Express
Galahad's Castle
The Loch Ness Horror

THE SHERLOCK AND LUCY SHORT STORIES

Flynn's Christmas
The Clown on the High Wire
The Cobra in the Monkey Cage
A Fancy-Dress Death
The Sons of Helios
The Vanishing Medium
Christmas at Baskerville Hall
Kidnapped at the Tower
Five Pink Ladies
The Solitary Witness
The Body in the Bookseller's
The Curse of Cleopatra's Needle
The Coded Blue Envelope
Christmas on the Nile
The Missing Mariner
Powder Island
Murder at the Royal Observatory
The Bloomsbury Guru
Holmes Takes a Holiday
Holmes Picks a Winner

Sign up at SherlockAndLucy.com
to stay up-to-date on Lucy and Sherlock adventures

THE **SHERLOCK HOLMES/
LUCY JAMES** MYSTERIES

GALAHAD'S CASTLE

BY **ANNA ELLIOTT**
AND **CHARLES VELEY**

This is a work of fiction. Names, characters, organizations, places, events, and incidents are either products of the author's imagination or are used fictitiously.

Text copyright © 2022 by Charles Veley and Anna Elliott
All rights reserved

No part of this book may be reproduced, or stored in a retrieval system, or transmitted in any form or by any means, electronic, mechanical, photocopying, recording, or otherwise, without express written permission of the author.

Typesetting by FormattingExperts.com
Cover design by Todd A. Johnson

"The very purpose of a knight is to fight on behalf of a lady."

Sir Thomas Malory
Le Morte d'Arthur, 1485.

Chapter 1: Watson

July 11, 1900

"It's called Galahad's Castle," the Pinkerton man said.

He unfolded a newspaper, spreading it across the wide mahogany table of the Diogenes Club library. The page in view showed a large sketch of a castle tower. Below it was a headline in bold type:

Chivalry Lives Again.

Holmes gave a grimace. We had come to the Diogenes Club quite early that morning at Mycroft's request. I had every hope that this case would be complex enough to catch Holmes's interest, for he had been out of sorts, as was usual when he was between cases. Now, from Holmes's reaction, it appeared we had not got off to a good start.

Across the table, Mycroft cleared his throat and said, "I promised Mr. Preston that we would give him a fair and respectful hearing. It is a matter of some delicacy."

Holmes leaned back in his chair, lowered his gaze, and steepled his fingers.

Preston nodded his thanks at Mycroft. He looked to be in his early thirties, with a lean, square-jawed face and penetrating blue eyes that darted quickly from Holmes to me and back.

He wore a corduroy jacket and, beneath his clean-shaven chin, a string tie made of rawhide, with a carved wooden effigy of a long-horned cow's head that took the place of a knot.

He continued. "The newspaper describes the project undertaken by the Earl of Tottenham to restore the castle, which he owns. At the moment, the castle's a wreck."

"The Earl is raising funds to restore it." Mycroft said.

Preston nodded. "The plan is to create a museum of sorts, modeled on King Arthur and his knights. Relics, suits of armor, that sort of thing."

"What does Pinkerton's care about restoring a castle?" Holmes asked.

"We don't. But we think Galahad is using stolen bonds to build his project."

"You represent the victim of the theft?"

I thought there was a barely discernible pause before the Pinkerton agent answered. "We're here to recover what we can."

"How much?"

"Three million. In bearer bonds. Unfortunately, they are perfectly anonymous—"

Holmes interrupted. "I am familiar with bearer bonds. Why do you think the owner of a British castle is using bonds stolen from your client?"

"Last week, our client received an interest coupon presented for redemption. The coupons are numbered, and our client identified it as having come from one of the stolen bonds. A British bank had already advanced cash on the coupon, and was now seeking to be made whole by our client."

"And the name of the bank?"

"The Tottenham Bank."

"And does the Earl of Tottenham have an account at the Tottenham Bank?"

Preston shrugged. "The bank won't confirm it. Client confidentiality and all that. But you'd think so, wouldn't you? Him being the largest local landowner and the bank being a local bank."

"Who issued the bonds?"

"The United States Treasury."

"Who presented the coupon to the Tottenham Bank?"

"The bank won't tell."

"Still, the coincidence is suggestive," Holmes said.

"There is more," Mycroft said.

Holmes cocked an eyebrow. "May I take it that Her Majesty's Government also supports the castle restoration?"

"Not necessarily. Though we could hardly oppose a monument to British heritage and chivalry."

"I see. You wish to avoid a scandal."

"We wish to maintain our cordial relationship with President McKinley's administration. But yes, we also wish to avoid having a British peer linked to a theft of such magnitude."

"You said there was more."

"The Earl's wife is American," Preston said. "She came to him with a substantial dowry last year."

I recalled the newspaper publicity regarding the wedding. The headlines referred to the bride as a 'dollar duchess.'

"How much dowry?" Holmes asked.

"One million dollars."

"And the bonds were stolen when?"

"Two years ago. Roughly seven months before the wedding."

"So some of the stolen bonds could have been the bride's dowry."

The American nodded. "Bringing them here removes them from our jurisdiction. If this was the US, we would have subpoena power. Here, we must depend on voluntary cooperation."

"Which you are not getting," Holmes said.

"Not as yet." Preston paused a moment, then leaned forward. "Look here, Mr. Holmes. I realize you don't know me from Adam, and that you've no reason to trust me, much less use your valuable time to help in this investigation. But—"

Holmes interrupted with an upraised hand. "I do not know you personally; so much is true. But I have in the past encountered and even collaborated with detectives from the Pinkerton's agency. There was Birdy Edwards in the Valley of Fear case."

The line of Preston's mouth tightened. "It was a shame what happened to Edwards. He was a good man."

"And then there was Leverton, who assisted in bringing the affair of the Red Circle to a satisfactory conclusion."

"Leverton?" Preston repeated. I thought his voice had a new and sharper undertone, though it was gone the next moment as he said, "Ah, yes. The hero of the Long Island cave mystery. Another solid agent."

Holmes studied him a moment, then nodded. "As you say. I know nothing of you, aside from the obvious facts that you were born in Tennessee, that in your youth, you have worked on both the railroads and the cattle ranches of the American west, that you are unmarried, and that you prefer cigars to a pipe. Apart from these facts, I know little about you personally."

There was a brief silence. The Pinkerton agent looked at Holmes, his mouth dropped slightly open.

Mycroft murmured, "Southern Kentucky, surely, not Tennessee. The accent is quite distinctive."

Preston closed his jaw with a click. "You're both right. I was born in Tennessee, then my folks moved to Kentucky when I was five years old."

Mycroft inclined his head in acknowledgment to Holmes, who answered with another nod before continuing.

"So, although I have no past experience in working with you, Mr. Preston, I do respect all that the Pinkerton's agency represents, and am willing to do what I can. As it stands now, there are three questions to be answered." He ticked them off on his fingertips. "One: does the Tottenham Bank possess your stolen bonds? Two: if so, are the bonds in the bank account of the Earl, via the dowry from his American wife? And, three: is the Earl rebuilding his castle with stolen funds?"

"Sounds about right," said Preston.

I had an idea. "I may be able to help with the bank," I said. "The vice president there is a patient of mine, and I have known him for a dozen years. Martin Huxley is his name, and he is an amicable chap—he helped me with a loan when I was first setting up my medical practice in Paddington. I might persuade him it would be in the bank's interest to cooperate, and that we would keep all information in confidence."

Preston nodded. "You can't do any worse than I did, that's for sure and certain."

Holmes said, "Thank you, Dr. Watson. Now, what do we know about the Earl?"

"Our London office gave us a file," said Preston. "The man is something of an eccentric. Intensely absorbed in medieval history and all things involving King Arthur. Sponsors archeological expeditions in Cornwall. Donates to the British Museum. He has recently changed his given name to 'Galahad.'"

"The noblest of Arthur's knights, as I recall," I said.

Preston had opened his mouth to reply, but at that moment one of the Diogenes Club servers approached with a slip of folded paper on a salver, which he held out to the Pinkerton's man.

Preston unfolded the slip and read it, a deepening frown between his brows.

"Not bad news, I hope, Mr. Preston?" Mycroft inquired.

"What's that?" Preston started, then folded up the paper again, seeming to come back from wherever his mind had been traveling. "No, no, nothing like that. Just an old—ah—acquaintance of mine. One I didn't think I'd get to see while I was here in London, but now it turns out that I'll be seeing after all." He rose from his chair and bowed. "Mr. Holmes, I thank you kindly for your help. We'll be in touch soon, then?"

"Just as soon as there are developments to discuss," Holmes agreed.

I thought he gave the American a keen look from under his lids, but he said nothing more, and after a moment's pause, Mr. Preston said, "Thank you again. I'll wish all you gentlemen a good day."

Holmes turned to me. "I believe our first line of inquiry ought to be the bank. Watson, perhaps you might use the Diogenes Club telephone to make an appointment with Mr. Huxley?"

I telephoned as Holmes had asked, but the results were utterly different from what any of us could have predicted.

Holmes took one look at my expression as I returned to our table and asked, sharply, "What has happened?"

I cleared my throat. "Huxley is dead, Holmes. The charwoman found him stabbed in his Tottenham office early this morning. Lestrade has asked us to come at once."

Chapter 2: Violet

Preston joined her even sooner than Violet had anticipated.

After leaving her message at the Diogenes Club, she walked a short way down Pall Mall to a small tea shop of the kind that seemed to breed like rabbits over here. Throw a stone from anywhere in London, and you were bound to hit some sort of establishment where the beverage of which the English were so unaccountably fond was served.

This particular shop was called *The Oriental*, and had walls painted a garish red and pots of bamboo in the corners. More to the point, it featured small alcoves for the tables, each screened off with a hanging curtain of cheap lacquered beads. A far cry from anything you would find in the actual orient, which she knew from personal experience since a case she'd been assigned to last year had taken her out to China.

That thought, though, made a hollow ache start throbbing under her ribcage, and what was worse, the now too-familiar feeling of being adrift, cut-loose and without purpose.

Since she was twenty, her entire life had been her career as an agent of the Chicago branch of Pinkerton's detective agency. Her every waking moment, her every scrap of energy had been dedicated to whatever case she'd been assigned. And now—

She snapped the thought off before her fingers could start curling or her pulse skipping. She needed above all else a clear and level head for the coming meeting with Preston—which wouldn't happen if she worked herself up into a pointless state of fury.

She breathed in, breathed out, ordering herself to refocus. At any rate, the tea shop struck a delicate balance: it offered a relatively private meeting place. But it was also public enough that however furious Preston might be, he wouldn't dare escalate to actual violence.

Not that she thought he was likely to attack her.

Well, she was fairly certain that he wouldn't go that far.

Violet had left the hanging screen to her own small alcove pulled aside so that she could maintain a watch on the front door, and she'd barely had time to sip the cup of coffee that the waitress had brought her before Preston came stamping in.

He must have been angry enough to walk straight out of his meeting with the Holmes brothers to the address she'd given him.

Or anxious to see her?

No, definitely angry. He was scowling blackly. Although the moment he caught sight of her, he rearranged his face into the smooth, deceptively affable expression she knew so well. The one that led women of all ages, from debutantes to grandmothers, to confide their deepest secrets in him, and even men to trust him with their lives.

"Is this seat taken?" He gestured to the chair opposite hers.

"Not at all. Help yourself."

Grimacing, he folded his long body into the chair, which was also made of bamboo and—Violet could personally testify—spectacularly uncomfortable.

"Thank you."

Violet eyed him warily over the brim of her coffee cup. "You're being extremely polite."

Preston raised one shoulder. "So are you. Although to be fair, the last time we saw each other, you threatened to shoot me in both kneecaps. So I guess we could only go up from there."

Violet almost choked, trying to smother a laugh. She didn't want to smile or laugh or find anything about Preston's company amusing or—heaven forbid—enjoyable. Heartily disliking him was safe; she would stick to that.

"Not necessarily. I could have made good on the threat and actually shot you in both knees."

He cocked an eyebrow at her. "You're surely welcome to try. Although I gotta warn you, they frown on that sort of thing here. A very law-abiding people, the English. I doubt you'd find British prison very enjoyable."

Violet put her head on one side, considering. "I don't know; it might be worth it."

Preston leaned towards her across the table, his tone altering. "What are you doing here?"

She really had gotten under his skin; it wasn't like Preston to ask obvious questions.

She arched an eyebrow in return. "You already know the answer to that, you just don't like it." Before he could respond, she asked, "How was your meeting with the Holmes brothers?"

Preston had himself back under control. His smile was more a baring of teeth than a gesture of anything like genuine friendliness, but his voice was perfectly level as he said, "Done your research, I see."

That was a deliberate jibe. They both knew that if she'd spent less time and care in making sure that her background research was solid and more time leaping headlong into action as Preston was prone to do, the outcome of the last case they'd both worked for Pinkerton's might have been very different.

Preston might not have been the one to walk away with a promotion and a hefty bonus in his bank account, for one thing.

She might still be employed, for another.

Violet raised her coffee cup to her lips and made sure that her voice was as level as his. "Always. So how much did you tell Mr. Holmes about the theft of the bonds?"

Preston raised one shoulder. "As much as he needs to know."

"Meaning as little as possible."

She thought there was a brief gleam of humor in Preston's gaze at that, but he only shrugged again. "This isn't a question of tailing the straying husband in a divorce case. It's national security. Mr. Holmes speaks highly of you, by the way."

"How kind of him."

"Yes, I hadn't realized that you'd met before. I'm surprised you didn't renew old acquaintance by joining us for today's meeting."

The truth was that she might have approached Sherlock Holmes directly, if Preston hadn't beaten her to it. Meeting Mr. Holmes again would involve some probably tedious explanations and possibly a lie or two, but she would have made them if not for Preston.

"So that you three gentlemen could studiously ignore the poor helpless female in the room—or you could generously offer to let me play second fiddle to you?"

"How do you know? Maybe I'd have offered to split my fees with you fifty-fifty."

Violet laughed outright at that. "Nice to know that if you ever decide to quit detective work, you can always go into a career as a comedian."

"Why not? We're colleagues, after all."

"No we're not. Not anymore."

Preston's gaze darkened. "I was against your being let go like that. I argued—"

She liked Preston much better when he was being deliberately maddening or provocative. His sympathy felt like sandpaper being scraped against an already raw wound.

"I don't need your help," she snapped. "I'm doing just fine."

"So I see." Preston looked her up and down. "Care to tell me who your current client is? Someone with enough money to pay your fare over here, obviously."

An image of her employer's face flashed into her mind's eye, juxtaposed momentarily with Mr. Pinkerton's. And a voice in the back of her head dredged up the old saying about better the devil you know than the one you don't.

Violet ignored the voice and reached for calm, pulling it on the way she would a change of disguise. Luckily for her, it was a skill she'd cultivated ever since she could remember.

There had to be some advantages to surviving a childhood like hers.

"I'd tell you, but then I really would have to shoot you."

The gleam of humor in Preston's gaze was more pronounced this time. But then he leaned towards her across the table again. "So if we're not colleagues and we're definitely not collaborating, why ask to meet up like this? If you hadn't sent me that note, I'd never have even known that you were in London."

Violet felt a brief and maddening flicker of satisfaction that he rated her skills that highly, but she squashed it. She didn't care what Preston thought of her, good, bad, or indifferent.

"Ground rules," she said out loud. "I thought we could set some."

Preston's eyebrows edged upwards. "Ground rules?"

"Just the one rule, really. We're both going to be trying to recover the stolen bonds. I'll agree to stay out of your way if you stay out of mine."

Preston's intense blue eyes held hers for a long moment, then he gave a fractional nod. "All right. May the best man—ah, that is, the best person win."

Violet stood up to go. "Don't worry. I intend to."

Chapter 3: Watson

"Mind your step around his chair," Lestrade said.

I caught the familiar coppery scent of blood.

Inside the banker's office, the heavy velvet drapes on one of the two tall windows had been partially opened. A shaft of daylight came through, gleaming on the spines of books and ledgers shelved on the back wall.

Holmes strode quickly to the side of the enormous desk. Lestrade followed.

I waited, observing the lifeless figure before me, hoping not to miss any clue. Huxley was in his shirtsleeves. He sat slumped forward, face down on the wide green blotter that nearly covered the surface of his desktop. What I could see of his normally well-combed brown hair was a disarrayed tangle. His starched white collar was blotched with a crimson stain, as were the sleeves and cuffs of his white shirt.

The ornate hilt of a silver dagger protruded from his neck.

Coming closer, I saw that Huxley's right index finger had been dipped in his own blood and apparently used to write three words on the otherwise empty desk blotter.

For my sins.

I felt an involuntary shudder of revulsion. The words seemed to add insult to his murder.

Holmes said, "He could not possibly have written this message. His murderer held his hand and traced out the words, dipping the fingertip into the pool of blood from time to time, as one would dip a quill pen into an ink bottle."

"What sins?" asked Lestrade.

Holmes ignored the question. "The murderer stood behind Huxley and stabbed the dagger into his neck," he went on. "Now, Watson, would you kindly give your medical impressions based on what you see?"

I stepped behind the desk, somewhat relieved to take on the role of objective observer. Careful to stand just outside the bloodstained area at the base of the chair, I examined the wounds on both sides of the neck. I noted that the blade of the dagger was nearly eight inches long.

"The initial stabbing blow hit a blood vessel," I said. "The flow from the wound issued rapidly. Blood pooled in the man's lap and onto the seat of the chair, and the overflow passed down the chair frame onto the carpet. The murderer waited, and then pressed the point home, severing the spinal column."

"As is apparent from the protruding tip of the dagger," Lestrade said. "But how do you know the murderer waited?"

"By the amount of blood. When the spine was severed, Huxley's heart would have stopped. The flow of blood would have stopped as well. There is a substantial amount of blood, so the heart was beating for more than a few moments."

"Why would Huxley not struggle when the knife made the initial wound?" Lestrade asked.

"Observe the hair at the crown of the skull, bunched up in disarray, whereas on the side it remains combed and sleek with brilliantine. His murderer grasped his hair from behind, pulled him erect, and struck with the dagger almost simultaneously. He may well have struggled initially, but the shock of the wound and the loss of blood would rapidly make him weak."

"Huxley must have known the attacker," Lestrade said. "Otherwise, he would not have permitted the man to take him from behind."

"Or perhaps he did not see his attacker until it was too late to defend himself," I put in, noting the heavy drapes behind Huxley's desk.

Holmes shrugged. "More importantly, there are several questions which must be answered–"

The office door opened, and a harsh voice interrupted. "What questions?"

The speaker was a distinguished, grey-haired chap, dressed in formal banking attire. His dark eyes flashed beneath bushy white brows.

The constable looked apologetically at Lestrade. "Sorry for the interruption. This gentleman says he's the president of the bank."

"I am Robert Sherwood. President here for the past twenty-two years," said the grey-haired man. "Now, I understand that you are Inspector Lestrade, and that you are Sherlock Holmes. And you, sir–" he said, looking at me–"must be Dr. Watson."

"Correct all around," Holmes replied.

"I also understand that Huxley wrote a suicide note in his own blood."

"Not correct," Holmes said. "He was murdered. Someone else wrote the note."

"Well, that's a relief."

"Sir?" Lestrade looked puzzled.

"Doesn't do for a bank officer to commit suicide. Makes people think he's hiding something."

"Who would benefit from his death?" asked Lestrade.

"I am about to retire next month," Sherwood said, "and Huxley would have moved up to my position. Though the presidency of this bank is hardly worth killing for. When did he die?"

Lestrade consulted his pocket notebook. "Sometime between five o'clock yesterday, when he had completed his last appointment, and five-thirty this morning, when the charwoman found his body here and telephoned Scotland Yard."

"Why did the charwoman wait until this morning?" Holmes asked.

"She thought he was working late and did not wish to disturb him. His door was shut."

"Did Mr. Huxley often work late?" Holmes asked.

"It was a habit of his," Sherwood said. "He had no wife to go home to. Now, what were those questions you referred to, Mr. Holmes?"

Holmes spoke in his usual rapid-fire fashion, ticking off the points of inquiry with his bony fingers. "One: You will notice the desk is clear. Was he in the habit of sitting at an empty desk?"

I knew the answer to that one. Huxley had been a copious note-taker when I had been with him in this office twelve years ago. I remembered him jotting rapidly into a ledger-style notebook with a quill pen, and occasionally burrowing into a stack of documents to retrieve a paper. But Holmes was speaking, and I did not interrupt.

"If not," Holmes continued, "what was ordinarily on his desk during a workday, and where are those materials now? I would expect his secretary may be helpful on this point. He has a secretary?"

Sherwood nodded. "Mrs. Clair. Solid, capable woman. She should arrive soon. Be a shock to her, I'll be bound."

Holmes continued, "Two: this dagger, the murder weapon. Was it normally on his desk—used as a letter opener, perhaps?"

I tried to recall if I had seen the dagger years earlier, when I had applied for my loan. I could not.

"Mrs. Clair would know. But I wouldn't want her to see it there in his neck," Sherwood said.

"She won't," Lestrade said. "The dagger will remain where it is until the mortuary examination."

"Mrs. Clair can tell us whether he kept such an object," Holmes said. "Now, finally, Mr. Sherwood, where is Huxley's appointment book, and who were his visitors yesterday?"

"I'll have Mrs. Clair brought in as soon as she arrives," Sherwood said.

"I shall need to interview the other bank employees as well," Lestrade said. "A room for the purpose would be helpful."

"You shall have my office for that," Sherwood said. "Will all three of you be staying?"

Holmes shook his head. "Dr. Watson and I have another engagement. Mr. Sherwood, I must leave you in Inspector Lestrade's most capable hands. Inspector, please do keep me informed as you require."

He then whispered something to Lestrade that I could not make out. Thereupon, he strode from the office.

I followed. On the pavement outside the bank, we flagged down a four-wheeler. Holmes directed the cabman to our address on Baker Street. I looked at my watch. It was not yet nine o'clock.

Inside the cab, I turned to Holmes.

"You have another engagement?"

Holmes drew a breath and gave me one of his overly patient looks. "An American. He made the appointment yesterday. He is concerned for the safety of his daughter, who has married a London nobleman. No, he did not say which nobleman."

He sat back and lit his pipe. I opened the window on my side of the cab. He fanned away some of the smoke. "Have no doubts," he said. "The death of your patient and friend will not be forgotten. We shall take up the case as soon as I have evaluated this American's fears for his daughter. And I shall telephone Lucy as soon as we return to Baker Street."

I asked, "What did you whisper to Lestrade?"

"I told him to search for a bloodstained towel."

And with that, Holmes closed his eyes. He remained silent until we returned to Baker Street.

* * *

When we were settled in our sitting room, Holmes telephoned Lucy James, his daughter and frequent co-investigator on our cases.

For a few minutes he explained the details of Huxley's death, and the Pinkerton man's idea that stolen United States Treasury bonds were being used to restore the castle owned by the Earl of Tottenham, via the dowry from his American wife. Then he said, "Pinkerton's London office provided a file on the Earl, the man who calls himself Galahad."

A pause. Then, "Yes, I have a copy. The man is respected by most, feared by some. Intensely absorbed in medieval history and all things involving King Arthur ... No, more than a dilettante. He sponsors archeological expeditions in Cornwall.

Donates to the British Museum ... He is feared because his supporters are vigilantes. They call themselves the Knights of Galahad and claim to be defenders and protectors of womanhood ... No, not bodyguards. Their protection takes the form of brutal retribution to discourage future abuse. Some husbands have been hospitalized; others have been crippled for life. Galahad himself stays above the fray ... No, the police turn a blind eye."

Holmes listened for a brief interval. Then, "Yes, the Galahad's Castle in the newspaper ... Yes, an expensive hobby indeed. Requiring a bank loan, we believe. Also, very possibly the use of the stolen bank notes sought by Pinkerton's. Either or both may connect to Huxley's murder, so ... yes, of course. I know you will."

He listened again and then gave Lucy the address in Tottenham where Huxley had lived. A moment later he said, "That is satisfactory," and hung up.

"Lucy will go to Tottenham immediately," he said. "She will call here this evening to report and make further plans."

CHAPTER 4: BECKY

"So Lucy's off investigating this Huxley's murder?" Flynn asked.

They were sitting in the kitchen at home, with the dog Prince asleep across the hearth. Flynn had knocked on the door a few minutes ago, and Becky had brought him back here to sit at the big oak kitchen table.

He'd been growing lately, his arms and legs looking even longer—and skinnier—in his ragged trousers and tattered corduroy jacket. Becky was fairly sure he didn't get any kind of regular meals, although he never admitted to being hungry, any more than he'd accept a place to stay with a roof over his head.

But he'd consented to share her toast and marmalade and eggs when she'd said she hadn't eaten breakfast yet.

"Yes." Becky made a face around a bite of scrambled eggs. She was sorry that Dr. Watson's friend Mr. Huxley was dead, but that didn't make her like being left behind here at home with nothing to do any better.

Jack was at work at Scotland Yard, and Lucy—

"Lucy had to go out to speak with Mr. Huxley's landlady," she told Flynn. "To find out whether she knows whether Mr. Huxley came home at all last night, whether he had any mysterious visitors, all of that sort of thing."

"And she didn't take you with her?" Flynn asked, spreading more jam on his bread.

Becky frowned harder. Usually, Lucy did let her come along on interviews with a murder victim's domestic staff. "Mr. Huxley's housekeeper apparently hates children," she said. "It was one of the conditions of her working for Mr. Huxley. She only works for men who are bachelors, with no wives, children, or pet animals in the house."

"Sounds like a laugh a minute," Flynn said. "Maybe Huxley got himself murdered just to get away from her."

"It would have been easier to just fire her; it's not as though they were married," Becky pointed out. "We're supposed to go over to Baker Street this afternoon at five o'clock, by the way."

That was some consolation, at least.

"We can hear about anything that Lucy has uncovered, and get instructions from Mr. Holmes, if he has any assignments for us—"

She stopped at a ring of the front doorbell. Prince sat up with a snuffle and a low woof, and Flynn raised his eyebrows, instantly alert.

"Are you expecting anyone?"

"No." Anyone with a delivery would come around the back. Lucy wouldn't have returned already, and anyway, she wouldn't ring the bell.

Becky tiptoed quickly but quietly to the door and peered out through the peephole that Mr. Holmes had had installed along with all their other security measures.

A slim, dark-haired woman of around thirty stood on the front step. She wore a neat green tweed coat and skirt and carried a notebook and pencil in hand.

Becky hesitated. The woman looked harmless enough. But then, so did Lucy, and anyone who underestimated Lucy in a fight rarely walked away unharmed.

On the other hand, Becky would never find out who the woman was and what she wanted if she didn't open the door and talk to her.

Flynn had followed her into the front hall from the kitchen. Becky turned to him and whispered, "Stay out of sight, but be ready to follow my lead, all right?"

She barely waited for Flynn's confused nod before turning back to unlock and open the door.

"Hello there." The woman gave her a bright smile. She was quite pretty, Becky decided, with big dark eyes and long lashes and a face that she'd sometimes heard described as having a Spanish kind of beauty: red lips, high cheekbones, and a thin straight nose.

Becky was a fairly good judge of smiles, too, and this woman's looked genuine enough. Still, she wasn't planning to relax her guard.

"I'm with the census bureau," the dark-haired woman said. "We're taking a survey of everyone who lives on this street."

"Oh, really?" Becky pasted on a smile of her own. "Have you done the Harrisons yet? They live two doors down. If you haven't, you'll need a whole page of your book to write down all of them!" She made her eyes wide. "They have *ten* children! The oldest is my age, and the youngest is just a baby."

"Yes, that's right. The Harrisons." The woman consulted a page in her notebook. "Number 18."

Well, that settled that. Becky pretended to shift her weight from foot to foot, although really what she was doing was taking a firmer hold on the doorknob, in case she had to slam the door in the woman's face. "What is it you want to know?" she asked.

"Just how many people live here, and their names and occupations," the woman said.

"Their occu—" Becky trailed off, frowning as though in confusion. "I think you'd better talk to my mother." She leaned her head inside the door frame to shout. "Mum! Mum! There's a lady here wanting to talk to you! Have you got time, or is Freddie still being sick all over the floor? Freddie's my little brother," she added, with a confiding glance back at the dark-haired woman. "Mum says he must have eaten too many green apples yesterday. Or else it's something catching, you never know."

The woman's smile wavered briefly. "I ... ah ..."

Flynn's voice interrupted from inside the house. Becky could imagine he'd have something to say later about being forced to pretend to be her mother. But the words were pitched high enough to sound more or less like a woman.

"Not now, I'm busy! Tell her to come back later."

"All right." Becky leaned on the door frame and gave the woman an apologetic smile. "I suppose you'd better come back after Freddie is done being sick. Unless it is something catching, then maybe you don't want to."

As she spoke, she clicked her fingers behind her back. For months, now, she'd been training Prince for occasions just like this. The big dog obeyed the summons right away, padding to join her in the doorway. And as soon as he spotted the strange woman on the front step, he let out a loud, angry bark and a threatening growl.

He wasn't acting. Becky had also trained him to attack on command, but he really didn't like the look of the dark-haired woman.

Becky put a hand on his collar and made a show of trying to pull him back while he snarled and lunged.

"Sorry!" she shouted above the noise of Prince's barks. "He doesn't like strangers. I'd better get him back inside."

With a final tug, she pulled Prince back, closed the door behind them and snapped all the locks into place, and added the security chain, besides.

"What's that all about?" Flynn asked, coming out from where he'd been hiding around the corner in the front room.

"Shhh!" Becky hissed. "No time. Quick, out the back way."

Prince didn't think much of being left inside, but sat down on his haunches in the middle of the kitchen when Becky ordered him to stay. She wasted a few precious seconds retrieving the back-door key from its hook on the wall and locking the door behind them, but that couldn't be helped.

"I don't think she'll try to break in," she murmured to Flynn as they crossed the walled-in courtyard that opened off the kitchen. "She's seen Prince, and as far as she knows, we're still at home. But better to be safe."

She led the way around the side of the house, flattening herself against the wall to be as invisible as possible as they approached the road.

The street was busy at this hour of the morning, with carriages bringing men to work at their offices or ladies to their friends' houses for coffee. Delivery vans rumbled by, pedestrians pushed and jostled, and for a moment, Becky was afraid that the dark-haired woman was already out of sight.

Then she spotted the back of the woman's dark hair and green tweed suit a block up the road, threading her way through the traffic at a brisk pace.

"Come on!" she told Flynn. "Hurry!"

They darted after the woman, earning several dirty looks from passers-by whom they narrowly avoided bumping.

When they were ten or twenty yards behind the woman, Becky judged it safe enough to slow to a walk.

"You planning on telling me who this woman is and why we're following her?" Flynn asked, catching his breath.

"I can't tell you who she is, because I don't know," Becky said. "But as for why we're following her, she claimed she was taking a census survey."

Flynn made a disparaging noise. "Everyone and his brother uses that old story. You'd think if she had brains she could have done better than that."

"I know." Which was odd, because Becky hadn't gotten the impression that the woman was stupid. "Then I asked if she'd already called at number eighteen, where they have ten children."

Flynn's look of long suffering vanished, and he looked instantly alert. "Number eighteen is an old retired army colonel and his wife. No kids."

"I know. That's why I picked it." Becky dodged around a shoe-shiners stall that had set up camp in the middle of the pavement and kept moving, keeping her eyes on the dark green tweed suit jacket ahead of them. "If the woman were honest, she would have corrected me, or she could have said that she hadn't been to number eighteen yet. But she pretended to check her records book and agreed."

"Not very creative in the lying department *and* not too good at thinking on her feet."

"I don't know," Becky said. "It could just be that she's used to thinking children are too stupid to tell when someone's lying."

Usually Becky resented the way adults tended to view children as having only half a brain. But Lucy always said that getting your opponent to underestimate you meant that the fight was already halfway won.

Ahead, the dark-haired woman turned a corner onto a narrow side street.

"Hurry, we can't lose sight of her," she said.

"Should be all right; she's not that far ahead." Flynn sped up his own pace to match hers, though. They rounded the corner and—

Becky's stomach dropped. "She's gone."

The street was a quieter one, empty of traffic except for an elderly street sweeper pushing a broom through the dust at a crossing, and a troop of midget acrobats who were just setting up camp on the corner.

"How'd she disappear that fast?" Flynn asked.

Becky scanned the street. "She could have ducked into one of the buildings along here."

The street was mostly a residential one, with narrow brownstone town houses crowding together. But there were a few businesses: a milliner's shop, a shoemaker's, a greengrocer's, and a bookseller.

"All right, let's have a look," Flynn said.

They peered into the windows of all four shops, but didn't see any sign of the dark-haired woman.

"Doesn't necessarily mean anything," Flynn said. "She could have gone straight through and out through the back of any of them. Do you want to go in and ask around? Or try knocking on some doors?" He gestured to one of the townhouses.

"Right, and we can tell people we're taking a census survey?" Becky said sourly. She blew out a breath. It annoyed her that they'd lost the dark-haired woman, but it wasn't Flynn's fault.

"I don't think we'd better start asking questions," she said after considering for a moment. "If we do—and if she has contacts with anyone on this street—word could get back to her that we were trying to find out more about her. Right now, she doesn't know that we suspect her. I think maybe it's better to keep it that way until we find out more."

"And we find out more how, exactly, without investigating?"

"I didn't say that we shouldn't investigate, just that we shouldn't ask questions right here and now," Becky said. "First of all, does anything strike you as interesting about the timing of her coming around?"

She turned around, starting to make her way back down the street. Flynn fell into step beside her.

"You mean the fact that she showed up on the morning that Huxley's murder was discovered?" he asked.

Becky nodded approval. That was the good thing about Flynn. He might argue and complain about some of her ideas, but when it came to thinking about a case, their minds worked very much alike. "Exactly. It could be just a coincidence."

"But not likely."

"No. I think she's connected somehow to the case of Huxley's murder, and came to find out how much we—and Mr. Holmes—know about it."

Flynn had his hands in his pockets, scuffing his boots through the dust and debris that had piled up along the edge of the pavement. "Think she's the killer? You got a better look at her than I did."

Becky frowned, trying to call up the details of her encounter with the dark-haired woman. "I don't know. She was friendly with me. But I think she could be ruthless, if she had to be. And she's strong, too. Thin, but strong. There's one other thing, too: I overheard Lucy speaking to Dr. Watson on the telephone before she left. According to him, it looks as though the killer was someone Mr. Huxley wasn't afraid of, because he or she got right up behind Huxley and stabbed him from behind."

"A young woman could fit that bill," Flynn agreed. "So how do we find out more about her?"

"Tottenham is only about half an hour from here by train, if that," she said. "And Mr. Huxley lives nearby; I overheard Mr. Holmes giving Lucy the address."

"And what do we do if Lucy's still there, talking to Huxley's housekeeper?" Flynn asked.

Becky waved that away. The buried fear that had been nagging at her all morning rose up in full force, knotting her stomach.

It wasn't just that she hated not being included in an investigation. She also hated the thought that something might happen to Lucy when she was off on her own. Lucy was clever and brave and strong, but even she needed someone to watch her back.

"Lucy will probably be gone by the time we get there. And anyway, we won't actually go in, just have a look around. Our cover story will be easy, too. Sir Galahad is putting on a fair near the castle; I saw a newspaper article all about it. Games and amusements and even a steam-powered carousel."

That had been another—albeit minor—reason that she'd resented being left behind today. A murder investigation was far more exciting than a fair any day. But she'd also never been on a carousel ride before.

"Anyone who sees us will assume that we're just two more children visiting the fair."

"Yes …"

Flynn still sounded doubtful, but Becky ignored the hesitation in his voice. "If we leave now, there's plenty of time for us to get to Tottenham, have a look around at Huxley's house and up at the castle, and then be back at Baker Street by this afternoon to meet with Mr. Holmes."

Chapter 5: Watson

"I'm Jonas Brown, and I'm worried about my little daughter, Mr. Holmes," said our American visitor, as he entered our sitting room.

Indeed, the man did appear in considerable disarray. Stains discoloured his badly trimmed grey goatee and moustache. The brim of his battered grey fedora sagged above his wispy grey hair, which also needed a trim. His tan walking coat hung unbuttoned, revealing a dingy green-checked vest and allowing his capacious round middle to protrude. His American-style boots bore mud stains. If this was an American millionaire, I thought, he was an eccentric one.

"Pray take a seat and compose yourself," Holmes said. "We have coffee—"

Brown shook his head.

"And you're Dr. Watson, I suppose. Two single fellows. You don't know what it is to have a daughter." His eyes, reddened and rheumy, squinted first at Holmes and then at me. "Am I right?"

I was not about to reply.

"The statement may or may not be true," Holmes said, "but it is quite irrelevant. Now, you appear to have spent the better part of the morning wandering the streets. Is that correct?"

Brown gave a knowing look. "I see what you're up to. You answer my question with another question. Okay, maybe I'll just take a cup of coffee after all. And incidentally, yes, I was wandering about. I was trying to clear my head."

I poured coffee from our table brought it to him. He lowered himself onto our settee and sipped.

"I can't take much time here," he said. "Got a train to catch. Going back to the states tomorrow. Lots of loose ends to tie up."

Holmes nodded.

"So. About my little daughter. She's what you Brits call a 'dollar duchess.'"

"The term is a familiar one," Holmes said.

"Shows weakness in the American character, I say. Our women think marryin' some British duke or other will do 'em some good, just because they'll get a title, which is nothin' but a bunch of words, but they're willin' to pay out good money—"

"Mr. Brown," Holmes interrupted. "Please be brief."

A resentful look from our client. Then a nod. "Yeah, well, I do have that train to catch. Anyway, the dollars came from me. I plunked down a cool million of 'em, Mr. Holmes."

"A million in cash?"

"Gilt edge bonds. From my portfolio. All blue chip companies. Good as cash. Dowry so my daughter could marry this aristocrat—"

"Who, precisely?"

"Named Trent. In Tottenham."

My eyes widened. This could not be a coincidence, I thought.

"Big shot peer of the realm, with a castle and all," Brown continued. "But it's all a sham, tumbledown affair; the Earl's a fool about it."

Holmes kept his face expressionless. "In what way is the Earl a fool?"

"That heap of rocks is a financial sinkhole, Mr. Holmes. Not fit to live in, so now he's hired workmen to rebuild it, and not the sensible way, no, it has to be repaired just the way they did things in the stone age or whatever. And he won't stop there! No, he pays people to dig around it to look for King Arthur's grave and his armor and such. And not just in Tottenham. In Cornwall, too. And other godforsaken places. And that big museum here in London just adores him for sponsoring their boondoggle trips, and they give him ribbons and plaques for digging up a lot of rubbishy metal trinkets—and for all the donations he gives them, of course. He gets his name in the paper and they put him in their programs as a sponsor. All that money squandered, and all for his own vanity."

"How does your daughter feel about this, Mr. Brown?"

Brown grimaced. "She hasn't felt the pinch yet. Just now she's all a-twitter about the big event they're puttin' on this week."

"What event?"

"To dedicate the new name for the rock heap, Mr. Holmes. 'Galahad's Castle.' Folks will come from miles around, they tell me. A real lollapalooza."

"Fascinating," Holmes said, suppressing a yawn. "Why is a new name required for the castle?"

"Oh, didn't I tell you?" Brown's eyes twinkled with anticipation. "My fool son-in-law had his name changed to Galahad. So now instead of calling him 'Sir Roderick,' folks are obliged to call him 'Sir Galahad.' Now, don't that beat all?"

Holmes lit a cigarette.

"Anyway, all this folderol will make money, they say, and Lottie has high hopes." He paused. "Her mother would have loved it too, rest her soul. Just the stuff the ladies in Cleveland would rave on about and sail across the Atlantic to come visit. But, Mr. Holmes, her mother's not with us anymore, and Lottie—that's my daughter's name, Carlotta, and I call her Lottie—well, I've got to go back to Cleveland, and I can't be staying around here to protect her."

"Why should she need protection?"

The American's words tumbled out in a rush. "Because sooner or later the money's bound to run out and then this humbug Galahad is going to want another dowry to keep on with his tomfoolery, and that's when I think he's going to kill my daughter!"

Holmes waited for a few moments to allow the man's obvious emotion to subside. Then he said, "Can you tell me why you think that?"

"Because Trent's done it before. His first wife died about two years ago. She was American, too, and she had a million-dollar dowry as well. They called it an accident when she fell from a tower there. Nobody said boo. But it was all too convenient, if you ask me. He'd spent that first dowry, you can bet your boots on that, and when he needed more, he took the quick way."

"And yet you paid for your daughter's dowry?"

"I ask myself why I didn't look closer. But it's not like buying a railroad, Mr. Holmes. You have these women, chattering on, all happy and bright—anyway, what's done is done. That's why I come to you."

One of Holmes's tight little smiles appeared for a moment. "What would you have me do?"

"Two things. First, look into the death of that there first wife. Name was Rose. Bound to be records and such. If you can prove it was murder, then I can take Lottie away back to Cleveland.

She'll have to listen to me then, if you get the evidence. Then we'll be home and dry and done with all this hoity-toity business."

"And the second thing?"

"Protect Lottie, Mr. Holmes." Brown's voice quavered. "Protect my little girl."

Holmes stood up. "Mr. Brown, I regret that I can do neither of those two tasks."

"Why not?" Brown's moustaches and whiskers quivered above his outthrust chin.

Holmes waved a hand in a dismissive gesture. "I am not obliged to explain myself, Mr. Brown. I choose my own cases. Now, you had best go and catch your train."

Brown did not move. "My banker has ten thousand dollars of my money in escrow, ready to deliver to you as a retainer, Mr. Holmes. Non-refundable. All I have to do is tell him you've accepted."

Holmes shook his head.

"Very well, twenty thousand."

Holmes turned to me. "Dr. Watson, would you kindly assist Mr. Brown downstairs to his cab?"

"How do you know I have a cab?"

"Because I saw you arrive, and your cab is still at the curb." Holmes turned to our bow window, cutting off conversation.

I took a step towards Brown. Grumbling a bit, he stood.

I escorted him downstairs. On the pavement, Brown gave a curt nod to the waiting driver, who hurried to open the cab door. Then Brown turned to me.

"Holmes may change his mind."

"I doubt that very much."

"If he does, he'll want that retainer. He'll want it right away. My bank will send Holmes twenty thousand the minute Holmes asks for it. All he needs to do is call my banker. Here's the man's card."

So saying, he took a business card from his waistcoat pocket and pressed it into my hand. "You'll give it to Holmes, won't you?"

I took the card out of politeness and tucked it into my pocket.

"Thank you, Mr. Brown," I said. "I wish you a safe journey."

He got into the cab and clapped the door shut. The cab drove away.

My hand went to my pocket. I retrieved the business card Brown had left.

The card read: *Martin Huxley, Vice President, Tottenham Bank.*

Chapter 6: Watson

"I have summoned Lestrade," Holmes said. "We must report on the meeting with Brown. The connections with Galahad's Castle are beyond coincidence."

"And Huxley is Brown's banker," I added. "Or, he was."

A moment later we heard Lestrade ring our doorbell, and then he was in our sitting room. He had a leather-bound appointment book with him, and a piece of paper.

"Mrs. Clair gave me these," he said. "Why did you not tell me you were on retainer from Huxley's bank?" Lestrade thrust out his chin in an accusing manner. "You can see your name right here, in Huxley's note."

Debit Brown account to establish Escrow for Mr. S. Holmes. 10000 up to 20000 on retainer.

"When we last spoke," Holmes said, "I had not spoken to Brown. There was no retainer then, and there is none at present. As Watson will attest, I declined the two cases Brown requested I investigate."

"Brown gave me Huxley's card," I said, "hoping Holmes would change his mind."

"What two cases?"

"First, Brown wanted me to find evidence to convict his son-in-law of murdering his first wife two years ago."

Lestrade bridled. "That is a police matter, surely, and one

that a private investigator would have no authority to pursue."

"As I said, I declined," Holmes said.

"Why did Brown suspect his son-in-law?"

Holmes shrugged. "Brown made the dubious assumption that the Earl had squandered the dowry of his first wife and then killed her."

"Why?"

"To allow him to marry again and receive another dowry."

"Why would Brown think that?"

Holmes shrugged again. "If you wish to begin an inquiry, you have the authority …"

"Oh no. Not without evidence."

"Precisely. Now, Brown also feared that the present Lady Trent would meet the same fate as the first. That was the second case Brown wished me to take up: to protect Lady Trent from her husband. I declined, of course. I am not a bodyguard, and I have no idea whether Lady Trent would desire me to involve myself in a case that might pit me against her husband."

"You did not see Lady Trent?"

"Her father came here alone."

"Well, he brought her to visit Huxley yesterday."

Lestrade turned to the entry in Huxley's appointment book. "Mrs. Clair wrote this."

4:00. Mr. Brown and Lady Trent to see Mr. Huxley.

"Mrs. Clair said the tick mark shows that the appointment was kept. So, the daughter came with Brown to Huxley's office at four o'clock yesterday."

"Did anyone see them leave?"

Lestrade consulted his notebook. "The doorman at the bank says he saw Huxley walk through the bank lobby with an older man and Lady Trent just before five o'clock yesterday. Huxley hailed a cab for them. The doorman was a bit done up about it, since normally he would have hailed the cab and received a tip."

"Did the doorman see Huxley return to the building?"

Lestrade glanced at his notebook again. "My constable's report doesn't say. Just says the cab drove off with both the father and the daughter inside."

"Have you interviewed the staff at Trent Manor?"

Lestrade looked puzzled. "About what?"

"About when the father and daughter arrived. Did they go directly from the bank to Trent Manor? How far away is that, how much time would normally elapse if they did go directly, and how much time did indeed elapse?"

A shrewd look came over Lestrade's ferret-like features. "An alibi, you mean. They were among the last to see Huxley alive, so you're asking whether they have an alibi for the time of his death?"

Holmes nodded. "You will also want to ask the daughter about the interview with Huxley. Did he seem distraught? Did he mention any enemies who might wish him harm? That sort of thing. And the same questions to Brown, if you can find him before he sails for America."

"I have men on the lookout for Brown. I can't detain him, of course, but I can have him questioned."

"Do your men have a description of Brown?"

"We can get that from Mrs. Clair. She saw Brown and his daughter come in to Huxley's office."

"I will save you the trouble. Brown is an unkempt portly man of middle age who left here wearing a grey fedora, a rumpled tan coat, and muddy brown boots with lifted heels and toes pointed in the American style. His green-checked waistcoat was in need of a wash, as were his grey beard and moustache."

"Anything else?"

"Watson tells me that Huxley kept a notebook. Where is it?"

"We searched. So did the secretary, Mrs. Clair. It didn't turn up."

"The files of the loans and applications he was working on. Where are those?"

"Mrs. Clair said they were on his desk yesterday when she went home."

"Did you search beneath the window of Huxley's office?"

Lestrade pursed his lips. "For the missing items?"

"For a disturbance in the ground, indicating that items had been dropped from the window and then recovered."

The sigh Lestrade gave was answer enough.

"I must interview Mrs. Clair," Holmes said.

"She's not at the bank," Lestrade said. "Sherwood sent her home this morning after she spoke with me. Thought she should take the day off and rest, after such a shock."

Holmes's hawk-like features hardened. "Did she have a police escort?"

Lestrade gave a puzzled look. "Why would she need—"

Holmes picked up our telephone receiver, gave the generator crank a swift turn, and spoke. "Tottenham Bank. Office of the President. Mr. Sherwood himself. Immediately." Then he handed the receiver to Lestrade.

"When Sherwood comes on the line, find out where Mrs. Clair lives. Do not take no for an answer. Find out if she has a telephone. If she does, call her and tell her to lock her door and admit no one until she sees you and only you. If she has no phone, send a constable at once to stand guard until we arrive."

Lestrade stared, open-mouthed.

"Someone went to considerable trouble to remove all the records of Huxley's current activity. Mrs. Clair is the best source of the information needed to reconstruct those records. And the murderer was alone in the bank last night, with access to Mrs. Clair's desk and, presumably, to her home address."

He paused as Lestrade spoke to Sherwood's office.

After a brief conversation, Lestrade set down the receiver. "No phone. She lives at 236 Floral Street. I'll send a man from the Edmonton Station."

"I hope I am wrong," Holmes said.

Our cab arrived at 236 Floral Street fifty minutes later. As we got out, I saw two uniformed constables at either side of the front door.

Their grim expressions told us that Holmes had not been wrong.

Chapter 7: Lucy

Based on what I had heard of her character, I had formed a mental image of Mr. Huxley's housekeeper as a classic tartar: bony, hatchet-faced, and thin-lipped, with thin gray hair scraped back into an uncompromising bun. The woman who opened the front door, though, was so different from that mental picture that for a moment I wondered whether I was at the right address.

"Mrs. Lambe?" I asked.

"Yes, that's right." At first glance, Mrs. Lambe looked as though she could have modeled for an illustration of the fairy godmother in the Cinderella tale. She was tiny, the top of her head barely reaching to my shoulder, and she wore a pink tea gown spattered with a print of delicate white flowers and trimmed with lace at the neck and hem. She looked to be somewhere about fifty or sixty, but her small, pink-cheeked face was relatively unlined, and she wore her snowy white hair piled high in immaculate curls.

Her bright blue eyes looked me up and down, and then her small rosebud mouth pursed in the beginnings of a disapproving frown. "You're not one of those reporters, are you, like the other one? Because I will tell you straight out that I have nothing whatsoever to say—"

"I'm not a reporter, no. I've come to ask you a few questions about this sad affair of Mr. Huxley's death. I believe the police notified you that I would be coming?"

Her expression cleared. "Oh, I see. I do beg your pardon, I'm sure, but you wouldn't believe the trouble I've had with the newspaper reporters! Why, I found one of them rooting through the trash! Simply shameless, she was." Mrs. Lambe shuddered, then peered suspiciously down at my feet. "You don't have any mud or dust on your shoes, do you? You would not believe the state of the *boots* on all of those policemen who came to search poor Mr. Huxley's rooms. The dirt was simply *indescribable*! I've only just finished cleaning it all up."

To judge by her expression, the dirt had upset her far more than her employer's murder, but antagonizing a potential witness—especially this early in an interview—was almost never a good idea. I summoned up a smile. "I promise to wipe my feet very carefully on the mat."

Mrs. Lambe continued to stare at my shoes a moment longer, but then finally said, grudgingly, "I suppose that will be all right. I've spread out sheets of newspaper in all of the rooms to walk on—just in case the police have to come back. So if you promise to step only on those and *not* on the carpets, you may come in."

"Thank you so much."

The housekeeper led the way into the house, and I followed—taking care to walk as instructed on the sheets of paper that had been carefully laid out in a trail from the front door into the sitting room on the right.

The interior of the house was much what I would have expected: decorated in an old-fashioned style, and so spotlessly clean that I suspected even a single mote of dust or molecule of dirt would be terrified to show its face. The sofa and chairs were upholstered in glossy black brocade, the cushions all so uniformly smooth that they looked as though they had never been sat on since their arrival from the factory.

Nor, I noticed, did Mrs. Lambe invite me to sit down, but remained standing in the doorway, her back very straight and her gaze occasionally twitching to check whether I had taken a step off the protective layer of newspaper.

"What was it you wished to know?" she asked.

"When did you last see Mr. Huxley?"

"The day before yesterday, when he left to go to work at the bank." Mrs. Lambe's answer was prompt.

"Was he worried or upset at all?"

"Really, I couldn't say." She looked slightly surprised at being asked to consider the question of her employer's emotional state, as though she'd never thought about it before. "I served him his breakfast as usual. Eggs and toast. He particularly asked for toast." She sniffed. "Which was very inconvenient, because he would persist in scattering the crumbs all over the tablecloth. He ate, and then left at his usual hour of half-past eight o'clock."

"And you weren't alarmed when he didn't come home that night?"

"No, it was quite usual for him to work late sometimes and not return until after I myself had retired for the night. Or for him to travel into the city for a dinner engagement with friends or business associates."

I changed tactics. "Are you acquainted with Sir Galahad, up at the castle?"

"Only by reputation." Despite the negative answer, Mrs. Lambe's expression showed for the first time a spark of interest in something other than household cleanliness. "But he has caused quite a stir in the neighborhood. He and those knights of his, as he insists on calling them."

"Oh? How so?"

"Well." Mrs. Lambe lowered her voice conspiratorially. "Mr. Wells, who runs the Duck and Drake—that is the local public house—is known to be a very hard man, particularly when it comes to the treatment of his wife. I don't, of course, like to repeat *gossip*. But they say he has a terrible temper, and has even been known to—well, to strike her, when a fit of rage is upon him. Not that I'm surprised," she added darkly. "Before I came here to work for Mr. Huxley, I used to occasionally oblige by doing some cleaning work at the Duck and Drake, and I'm here to assure you, the state of the bar counter alone would be enough to give you nightmares. Sticky finger-marks everywhere, *and* peanut shells littering the floor, as likely as not."

From her tone, it was debatable which was the greater crime in Mrs. Lambe's eyes: mistreatment of Mrs. Wells, or peanut shells on the floor. Although even at that, hers was a marginally more balanced attitude than that of the law, which tended to turn an entirely indifferent eye on cases of domestic abuse.

"So this Mr. Wells is a wife-beater?" I asked.

"Well, yes," Mrs. Lambe agreed. "And I'm sure I'm not one to gossip, but I heard it just last month from Mrs. Carrington, who lives next door to the Duck and Drake, that Sir Galahad and his friends arrived at the public house late one night. They actually broke the door down, according to what Mrs. Carrington said, and dragged Mr. Wells out. They took him away, and no one knows what they did, but everyone agrees that he is quite a changed man, ever since. Afraid to so much as speak a harsh word to Mrs. Wells."

Mrs. Lambe's story cast an interesting light on Sir Galahad's character, but I couldn't for the moment see how it might apply to Mr. Huxley's murder. Unless—

"Did Sir Galahad ever have any quarrel with Mr. Huxley?" I asked.

"With Mr. Huxley?" Mrs. Lambe's eyes opened wide in astonishment. "Good gracious, no. I believe I heard that Sir Galahad had come to Mr. Huxley to apply for a loan, but apart from that, I should be surprised whether they had any contact between them at all. Why should you think there was a quarrel?"

"Well, if Sir Galahad and his knights have made it their mission to target men whom they believe have been disrespectful towards the women of the community ..."

Mrs. Lambe looked still more astonished. "But they can have heard nothing of that sort against Mr. Huxley! Why, he wasn't even married. And he was the gentlest soul alive—he wouldn't have hurt a fly, much less raised his hand in anger against anyone, man or woman. Although it is odd, your saying that."

"How so?"

"Well." Mrs. Lambe lowered her voice. "You asked before about Mr. Huxley being worried or upset. I didn't notice especially on the morning of the day he died. But a week or two ago, he came home very much out of sorts."

"Did he say what the trouble was?"

"He'd gotten an anonymous letter. Well, hardly a letter, just a note, at the bank. Just two words: *Die, sinner!*"

"Did he have any suspicions as to who could have sent the message? Had he any enemies?" I asked.

"Not that he mentioned to me."

"But he was frightened?"

"Well, not at first," Mrs. Lambe said. "He took it more as a joke, really—or some madman. But then he said he had begun to feel as though people were looking at him strangely when he went about town. Women especially. He said they were staring at him as though they held something against him. And that he distinctly heard one say, 'a wronged woman' behind his back."

"But he had no idea why public opinion should have turned against him in this way?"

"None. He was entirely at sea. But it worried him. He was a kindly man, Mr. Huxley." For the first time, Mrs. Lambe's eyes showed a glimmer of tears, and she dabbed at them with a handkerchief. "He was used to being respected and well-liked wherever he went."

"I'm sorry for your loss," I said gently. The truth was, at the moment I was as puzzled as Mr. Huxley must have been. Everything that Mrs. Lambe had told me had to be in some way related to Huxley's murder. But I couldn't see that the new information pointed to the guilt of any particular party—except perhaps one?

"Do you have the name of the local doctor?" I asked. "The one who attends Sir Galahad and his wife?"

"Yes, of course. That would be Dr. Norton. His office is on Clarence Road, near St. Anne's Church. You can't miss it."

Chapter 8: Watson

"For my sins?"

Seated behind his office desk at the Tottenham Bank, Mr. Sherwood looked bewildered. "Mrs. Clair's killer left the same message?"

"The same message as the one from Huxley's killer, yes sir," Lestrade said.

We had come to the bank from Mrs. Clair's small home, a five-minute walk. The scene was etched on my memory, and I felt the hot rush of outrage as I recalled how her body slumped over her kitchen table, her index finger stained with her own blood to write the message. Blood pooled on her chair and on the tile floor beneath. As with Huxley's fatal wound, Mrs. Clair had been held by her hair and impaled in her neck. But in this case, the weapon had been withdrawn and was not to be found inside the house. Lestrade's men had taken photographs. The local constables had made arrangements for transport to the mortuary. I had the frustrating sense that the murderer was mocking us.

"So, the same person committed both crimes," Sherwood said. His bushy white eyebrows were furrowed. A colourfully decorated model castle was positioned directly in front of him, at the center of his desk. The festive medieval-style banners seemed to clash with Sherwood's grim expression.

"There is another similarity," Lestrade said. "Mrs. Clair's belongings have been ransacked."

"What was taken?"

"At this point we have no one to tell us. We hope to interview friends or family, of course. But we need to find those people."

"You might start with the local church. She attended evensong regularly after work."

"Did Mrs. Clair take her work home with her?" Holmes asked.

"I very much doubt that," Sherwood said. "All her files were here in the bank. She occupied her free time with church and her sewing circle."

"And Huxley?" Lestrade asked. "Did he bring work to his home?"

"Quite possible. I believe Huxley spent most of his waking hours working."

"I'd better take a look, then." Lestrade said.

"I suggest another avenue of inquiry," Holmes said.

"What might that be?"

"Huxley's current work projects. The killer took his records from the bank, and ransacked Mrs. Clair's home, as if seeking relevant information. So, what projects was Huxley working on?"

Sherwood nodded in the direction of the model castle on his desk. "Our community project. Galahad's Castle. We were lending the funds for construction. The loan was up for approval at the next board meeting."

"It was viewed favorably by the bank?" Holmes asked.

"There's no certainty until the vote, of course. The board can't vote until it has the required documents before it, and those documents are missing. But I wouldn't have the model here in my office unless I supported the project."

"Who was the applicant?"

I was surprised at Holmes's question, for we both knew the answer, having been told in no uncertain terms by Mr. Brown. But I kept my features expressionless. Holmes, I thought, must have his reasons for not disclosing all we knew.

"The landowner is the applicant. Formerly known as Sir Roderick Trent." Sherwood gave a small smile.

"Surely he could duplicate his application materials."

"Well, he's somewhat disorganized. An eccentric fellow, as you might surmise. Calls himself 'Sir Galahad' now. I can't quite get accustomed to the change. But we can ask him. I'm sure he'll want to proceed with the project and won't want to lose any more time than can be helped."

I hesitated, wondering if we ought to mention the low opinion of the project held by Trent's father-in-law.

Then came a knock at Sherwood's office door. It opened to reveal a matronly woman in a black dress. "Mr. Sherwood?"

The bank president's grey eyebrows furrowed in annoyance. "I thought I told you no interruptions, Mrs. Leeds."

"I know, but this man says he needs to see you at once. He says it's extremely urgent."

"And please don't blame it on Mrs. Leeds, Mr. Sherwood." A man's voice, pleasant, friendly, apologetic.

Mrs. Leeds stepped inside, and I saw the speaker, a tall, dark-haired, handsome chap with a friendly smile and an almost boyish manner, dressed in light-coloured summer business attire. The smile seemed to disarm Mr. Sherwood.

"Ah, Calloway," the bank president said. "Enthusiastic as always. Are you sure you can't wait? I am very nearly done with these gentlemen."

"Oh? I hadn't realized. A thousand apologies, but I won't take more than a moment. I just want to implore you to bear with poor Galahad. He's very upset about Huxley, you know, and the shock of it just before tomorrow's celebration has made the strain worse for him." He paused, and his gaze seemed to take in all of us. "I see that castle model on your desk, Mr. Sherwood, and it gives me hope."

Lestrade stood up. "You know Sir Galahad, then?"

"I've been his friend for many years. I'm his man of business at times, and also his confidante."

"Then we shall want to interview you, Mr. Calloway. I am with the Metropolitan Police, investigating Mr. Huxley's death. These are my associates, Mr. Holmes and Dr. Watson."

The names did not appear to mean anything to Calloway. He merely nodded politely. "Happy to help however I can. I'm generally at the Castle, available at your service." He paused. "But Mr. Sherwood, may I take it that the construction loan is still under consideration?"

"For now, yes."

"That is all I needed to hear. I just wanted to reassure Galahad. I was afraid he might—well, no need to dwell on that. I'll be off now. Sorry again for the interruption."

And with that, he withdrew, followed by Mrs. Leeds.

Sherwood waited until the door had closed.

"I didn't like to tell him about Mrs. Clair," he said.

"Quite right, too," Lestrade said. "All in good time. At least this Calloway's willing to cooperate. Not sure about this Galahad and the rest of them at the castle, though. Aristocracy can be difficult and him being an eccentric aristocrat to boot will complicate matters. As a rule, the gentry seem disinclined to be open with the likes of us humble policemen. And in this case, we have no leverage—no evidence to connect them with Huxley's murder. Or Mrs. Clair's."

"Other than Lady Trent being one of the last to see Mr. Huxley alive," I pointed out.

"But that was in an ordinary business meeting, and Huxley was very much alive when her departure was witnessed," Lestrade said.

"There is also the difficulty of motive," said Holmes, "since the murders may delay the loan for the Castle restoration project. That result is quite the opposite of what Galahad appears to want, according to this Mr. Calloway."

"Well, of course, Galahad wants his loan," said Sherwood. "He applied for it!"

There was a moment's silence. Then Holmes spoke.

"Perhaps we can utilize Galahad's desire for the loan," he said, "if the bank will authorize it. I should like to bring in my associate, a young woman in whom I have the highest confidence."

Chapter 9: Flynn

Galahad's Castle wasn't far from the station. As soon as they got off the train, Flynn could see the stone towers on the horizon.

He shook his head in disgust. "Imagine being rich, and deciding to spend your money on a giant pile of a building like that."

The station was crowded with people in holiday clothes: mothers leading small children by the hand, and couples looking soppily at each other. The man and woman walking hand in hand up ahead of them were both wearing clothes so white Flynn would hate to see their laundry bill.

Becky frowned as they started down the road that led through the small village.

"Well, but I don't think Sir Roderick—or I suppose Sir Galahad is what he's calling himself now—actually bought the castle, just inherited it. Now he's run out of funds to fix it up the way he wants to. That's why he was applying to Mr. Huxley for a loan."

"That's even worse. Throwing good money after bad."

"What would you do with your money, if you were rich?" Becky asked curiously.

Flynn had never thought about it before. Sometimes he'd like a warmer coat or a better pair of boots. But things like houses and all the stuff that people filled them with—all that just weighed you down.

He shrugged. "Not build a moldy old castle, anyway, that's for sure."

The fair nearly covered the spreading lawn in front of the castle. There were booths for apple bobbing and dart throwing and other games, but the carousel was the main attraction, just in the middle of it all. It had a steam calliope blasting out music, and painted horses that rose up and down in time to the music as the whole thing spun around.

"Where do we start?" Flynn asked Becky above the noise. "Do we want to have a look around up at the castle?"

Becky wasn't paying attention, though. The carousel had slowed and come to a stop for all the riders to get off, and for a second, Flynn thought she was just staring at the painted horses like all the other kids in line hoping to get a ride on one.

But then he realized Becky was actually watching a little girl of four or maybe five, who'd just darted up onto the carousel's platform, not because she wanted a ride, but because she was chasing after a small tabby cat that had just leaped on, too.

"There's something the matter with that cat," Becky said. "Watch—it looks like it's ill or in pain."

Flynn peered more closely at the animal, which was weaving around the hooves of a horse painted in pink and gold. It didn't look healthy, that was certain. The cat was staggering unsteadily on its paws, looking like it was about to topple over.

"Almost looks like it's drunk," Flynn said, though his voice was almost drowned out by the squeals and shouts of the children who were now rushing to get on.

The kids all hopped onto horses, except for the little girl who was still chasing the cat as it staggered to and fro along the platform.

Becky watched with a worried frown. "Someone should tell the attendant not to start it spinning yet. She could get hurt."

She started towards the small booth at the side where a man in a striped pink shirt was working the levers that controlled the carousel, but too late. He'd already yanked the one that started the platform whirling and the horses bobbing up and down.

"Stop!" Becky raced forward, waving at the attendant. "You have to make it stop!"

Flynn didn't bother trying to follow her. Instead, he sprinted for the carousel, where the little girl who'd gone after the cat was now teetering on the edge of the platform, her arms whirling like a windmill as she tried to keep her balance.

He cupped his hands around his mouth. "Grab onto the—"

Horses, Flynn would have yelled to her. But the kid was too panicked—and maybe too young—to know what to do. The carousel sped up, spinning faster and faster, and it pitched the little girl off head-first. Putting on a burst of speed, Flynn just managed to catch her before she hit the ground.

"Hey!" The carousel attendant had finally noticed that something was wrong, and came running over to shout at Flynn, his pudgy face red with anger. "Get away from here! You can't be near the machinery while it's running!"

Flynn would have been all for ducking quietly away. He could care less whether or not the attendant thought he was a troublemaker.

But Becky faced the attendant, her hands on her hips. "He didn't do anything wrong! You're the one who started up the carousel while this little girl was still standing on the platform. She almost fell! She could have been badly hurt if Flynn hadn't caught her."

Flynn could have told her she was wasting her breath; he'd seen the attendant's type before, and years of experience with bad-tempered pub owners and cab drivers in London had taught him that you were better off running from fights with adults than trying to defend yourself.

If anything, the man's face got even redder. "Shut it, you!" He gave Becky a push that sent her stumbling back a step or two.

Flynn was still holding the little girl, but he set her down at that. Usually it was smarter to run, but then other times you ran into a real charmer like the attendant who needed a lesson in manners.

"Don't touch her!"

The attendant rounded on him and took a swing, trying to land a clout on Flynn's ear.

Flynn sidestepped, tripped the man over his outstretched leg, then elbowed him in the stomach as he went down.

The attendant landed on his fat bottom, his breath going out in a solid *whoof*. His face went from red to an unhealthy shade of purple, and he let out a roar of rage. Flynn braced himself.

"Forsooth!"

The man's voice, coming from directly behind Flynn, almost made him jump. "What manner of dispute mars the fairness of this bright day?"

Turning, Flynn found himself face to face with a tall, dark-haired man who could have stepped out of the pages of one of the history books that he'd seen on Doctor Watson's shelves. He was wearing green tights—Flynn had never seen a grown man wearing tights before—and a kind of short tunic, also green, but made of velvet and stitched with gold embroidery. It was broiling hot today, especially out here in the sun, but he still had a fur collar looped around his shoulders, and a big gold medallion sort of a thing hanging from a gold chain around his neck. A wide leather belt wrapped around his waist, holding a scabbard with a jewel-encrusted dagger.

Three men stood just behind him, all dressed more or less the same, except without the fur collar and wearing swords instead of daggers on their belts.

"Ah—" Flynn's jaw had dropped open, and it took him a moment to get his wits together enough to answer. Which meant that the carousel attendant got in first.

"This *boy*"—he said boy in the same way that Flynn had heard some people say *cockroaches*—"just pushed this child off of the ride."

Becky snorted and was plainly about to speak, but a red-haired woman accidentally bumped into her and almost dropped the melting ice-cream cone she was carrying.

"Oh, I do beg your pardon, I'm sure," the woman gasped. She was holding a white lace parasol to shade her face, and it kept bumping her in the head as she tried to juggle both it and the ice cream cone.

It was the female half of the couple from the train station, Flynn realized. The one whose snowy white clothes had caught his eye. Except now she had a big splatter of pink ice cream down her skirt.

"That's all right," Becky said automatically, not really looking because her attention was on Sir Galahad.

But while they were sorting themselves out and the red-haired woman was hurrying off again, the kid Flynn had caught piped up for the first time. Talking to the man in green.

"That's not true! *He* started the ride too soon." She jabbed a chubby finger in the attendant's direction. "I almost fell off, but *he* caught me!"

She pointed to Flynn, then finished by putting her thumb in her mouth and looking scared.

The man in green crouched down in front of her. For all he looked like someone who'd escaped from the loony bin, his voice was quite gentle and kind when he spoke to her.

"Don't be afraid, my dear. I am Sir Galahad Trent, lord and master of yonder castle." He gestured to the stone towers beyond the fair.

The kid stared at him, wide-eyed, but then took her thumb out of her mouth and whispered, "There was a cat. I thought it looked sick."

"A cat, you say?" Sir Galahad repeated, frowning. "Well, we shall certainly be on the lookout for the unfortunate creature. Neither man nor beast—provided they prove themselves of possessing a worthy heart—shall languish in need of aid in my domain."

The little girl kept staring at him, her jaw dropped slightly open, and Sir Galahad cleared his throat. "And now, my dear, where is your mother?"

"Over there." The little girl gestured. "She's serving tea in the Ladies' Aid Society tent."

"Good. Sir Lancelot." Sir Galahad turned to one of the other men dressed up like him. "Will you kindly escort this fair maiden back to her mother?"

Apparently they were all as crackers as their leader, because the other man bowed at the waist. "It will be my privilege, sire."

He held out a hand to the kid, and after a moment's hesitation, she took her thumb out of her mouth and let him lead her off towards the tea tent.

"Capital," Sir Galahad said briskly. "That part of our dispute is settled, then. Except"—he fixed the carousel attendant with a stern eye—"to deal with the knave who recklessly endangered a child's welfare, then saw fit to tell untruths about it in order to save his own unworthy hide."

Flynn understood about one word in ten of what Sir Galahad said, and to judge by his befuddled expression, the attendant wasn't doing much better. But he cringed in the face of the look that Sir Galahad was giving him.

"I was just …" he started to whine.

"Silence, varlet!" Sir Galahad bellowed. "You will remove yourself from my sight and my land at once, or I shall be forced to lock you in the dungeon and allow my magician to put a curse on you."

He gestured to one of the men behind him: the only one of the group who wasn't wearing medieval get-up. Flynn hadn't even realized that the fellow was one of Sir Galahad's band until that moment.

Somewhere around Sir Galahad's age—that was to say, in his 30's—the man had dark hair and a quiet, nondescript kind of face. He wore a fawn colored jacket and flannel trousers, and all in all looked the sort of fellow you could bump into on the street and five minutes later have a hard time recalling just what he'd looked like.

Although at the moment, he was looking acutely embarrassed at Sir Galahad's having singled him out.

"Isn't that right, Merlin?" Sir Galahad prompted.

Becky had been uncharacteristically quiet, but she couldn't let that pass. "Merlin?"

"Indeed." Sir Galahad made another grand, sweeping gesture. "Every court of Camelot must have its Merlin. Mine is well schooled in the magic of potions."

The dark-haired man looked even more uncomfortable. "I say, look here, we both know they're not potions. Not really, not any more than making a tincture out of willow bark for the sake of the salicin—that is to say, aspirin. Nothing magical about it."

Sir Galahad looked pained at the contradiction, but didn't argue. "In any case, the issue at hand is that this varlet must be removed from my sight!"

He nodded to another couple of his men—these in costume—who advanced on the carousel attendant and grabbed him by the arms.

The attendant didn't try to fight back or even resist. He looked as befuddled as Flynn felt, and allowed the men in costume to propel him away, frog-march style.

Flynn would have started sidling off then and there, but Sir Galahad swung around on him next, giving him a courtly bow.

"My congratulations, young sir. It is unusual to see the fair flower of chivalry so bright and alive in one so young. I salute you."

Looking around and trying to decide on what to say, Flynn happened to catch the eye of the dark-haired fellow. Merlin, although Flynn couldn't believe that was actually his name.

Merlin gave him a quick flash of a grin and a shrug—the kind of look that said that he knew as well as Flynn did that Sir Galahad was a bit off his onion, but what were you going to do about it?

Flynn was briefly grateful, but still couldn't come up with anything to say except, *Um.*

Lucky for him, Becky piped up again. "That's a beautiful dagger you have, Sir Galahad. Is it as old as your castle?"

Flynn, startled, shot her a quick glance. Becky was giving Sir Galahad her most wide-eyed, innocent look.

He beamed at her. "Even older, if you can believe that. 'Tis one of the relics that I have been fortunate enough to find in the course of my excavations here. Our excavations, I should say. Merlin oversees the majority of the work for me."

He glanced at Merlin again for confirmation, and the dark-haired man nodded, looking enthusiastic for the first time. "We've discovered the site of an eighth century hill fort that predates the castle by several centuries. It's been fascinating work."

Sir Galahad looked down with affection at the knife on his belt. "Yes, this dagger is only one of many remarkable weapons we've found. Although unfortunately, I have yet to entirely master the art of wielding either swords or knives in a true battle." He looked mournful for a moment, then turned back to Flynn. "But you, young sir. Can I offer you a reward for both your chivalry and for revealing to me the unscrupulous knave I had unknowingly allowed to remain in my employ?"

Flynn shook his head. "Ah, thanks, but I'm all right. Happy to help." He glanced at Becky. "We've got our train to catch."

"Then of course, I will not keep you. But I pray you will return soon, and enjoy all our fair kingdom has to offer." Sir Galahad spread his arms out to include the fair, the castle, and the surrounding land. Then he bowed. "Farewell, my young lord and lady, until we meet again."

CHAPTER 10: VIOLET

The children were going to be a problem. Walking away from the station beside the useful idiot whose acquaintance she'd made on the train, Violet acknowledged to herself that she had underestimated them rather badly.

Sherlock Holmes might be a man, but she had too much respect for his intelligence to try approaching him directly. Particularly given their previous acquaintanceship, even if those earlier encounters had been brief—and even if she'd assumed an entirely different persona than the one she was playing now.

But she thought she would be safe enough approaching the home of the young woman who—rumour had it—was Sherlock Holmes's daughter, even if they were careful never to publicize the family connection.

Well, that had been an error. She'd barely given the boy and girl the slip when they'd followed her back in London, and now here they were again in Tottenham.

"Don't you think, eh, what?" the useful idiot—whose name, as far as she could remember, was either Roger or Jerry—asked.

Violet paused to give him a vague smile and a murmur of assent, which she had discovered was all he appeared to require in a conversational partner.

Thin, with a narrow chest, heavily brilliantined hair, and a weak chin, Jerry—or possibly Roger—kept ogling her through his monocle and prattling on about horse racing and his yacht club and the dinners at his private gentleman's club in town, where someone named Squiffy had caused a scandal by getting roaring drunk and throwing boiled eggs at the waiter's head.

Violet had been listening to him throughout the entire train ride from London, and was beginning to regret her decision to use him for her own purposes by striking up an acquaintance. Particularly as Roger-or-possibly-Jerry seemed the type who would be difficult to get rid of again and would cling, limpet-like, oblivious of any hints she dropped about previous appointments or a pressing need to return to town.

But she'd spotted the two children—the boy and girl—boarding the train, and she hadn't wanted to take any chances. One of the first rules of throwing off a tail was to change not only your appearance but your company, if at all possible. It was amazing how many people wouldn't bother to look at the female half of a couple, simply because they were certain that the woman they'd been following had started out her journey alone.

She'd also changed her hair and clothes, but that added layer of protection was worth putting up with being alternately ogled and bored to tears.

She didn't feel particularly guilty about leading Jerry—or Roger—on, either. In her line of work, the ability to judge people at a glance tended to keep you breathing longer. Her temporary companion's plummy upper-crust accent and manners were entirely genuine, and his white flannel suit and cloth-topped boots were of excellent quality. But both clothes and boots were going shabby, and several bookmaker's slips had fluttered out of his pocket when he'd fumbled to find his ticket for the train conductor.

An impoverished aristocrat, trawling for a rich wife to restore his fortunes. Violet would stake her reputation on it.

"And here's the fair," he said, pointing to the array of brightly colored tents and crowds of holiday makers spread out before them. "Jolly things, fairs, what?"

"Jolly," Violet agreed.

Her eyes were already scanning the crowds of people, the muscles in her neck tensing in automatic anticipation of seeing a familiar face or a pair of broad shoulders.

"Do you?" Roger-Jerry asked.

"Hmmm—hmmmm," she murmured, wondering vaguely what it was she'd just agreed to.

She didn't see anyone she knew amongst the fair-goers. But she didn't relax. The way today was going, she wasn't betting on that remaining true for long.

Violet stole a quick glance over her shoulder, and was in time to see the two children approaching the carousel. She frowned.

"Here you are, then."

Beaming, Roger-Jerry presented her with a large cone of ice cream, which apparently she must have asked for without meaning to.

Violet suppressed a word that would undoubtedly shock her companion to his aristocratic core. That would teach her to let herself get distracted with thinking about Preston. The ice cream—of course it was pink strawberry flavor—immediately started dripping in a sticky mess all over her glove and the sleeve of her tea gown.

Now all the day needed to be truly complete was for Preston himself to turn up at this exact moment to see her getting coated in pink ice cream. She could just picture his slow, amused smile now.

"Oh, I see my friends over there." She gestured vaguely to a clump of people far away on the other side of the fairgrounds. "I'd better go and join them, but thank you so much for everything."

Leaving Jerry-Roger with his mouth still hanging partly open, she sped away.

Chapter 11: Lucy

My visit to Mrs. Lambe had given me a good deal to think about, so that it was several minutes after leaving Mr. Huxley's house before I realized that someone was following me.

In the past few decades since the advent of the railroads, Tottenham had transformed from sleepy, rural farmland into a bustling suburban town. Clarence Road, where Mrs. Lambe had directed me, was crowded with both carriages and pedestrians, housewives doing their daily shopping, and farmers bringing their cartloads of summer vegetables to the markets.

But I realized as I was passing by St. Anne's church that there was one particular set of footsteps behind me that seemed to pause when I paused, and speed up when I accelerated my pace.

Turning around would only alert whoever my follower was that I was aware of their presence, and giving up the element of surprise was never a good way to start a confrontation. Particularly since as far as I could judge from their sound alone, the footsteps belonged to a man of at least six-foot height, strong physical build, and an age somewhere under thirty.

St. Anne's was a pretty, stone-built church with a tall bell tower and gothic-style arched windows. I sped past the low stone wall flanking the narrow strip of lawn that surrounded the building, ducked behind the church apex, and waited. Here at the rear of the building there was no one else about, so I at least would have fair warning of anyone who followed me back—

Footsteps sounded from around the corner of the church's outer wall. I immediately pressed back against the stones behind me, taking quick stock of my available weapons. I had my Ladysmith pistol, but a gunshot here would likely draw a crowd, something I wanted to avoid. I settled for picking up a stray rock from the ground.

The footsteps drew nearer. A tall, dark-haired young man rounded the corner of the church. I'd already started to throw my rock, and only just managed to jerk my arm at the last second to re-adjust my aim.

The rock that would have hit the man's head glanced off his shoulder instead.

The man raised an eyebrow. "The next one kills me?"

"I hope not. Becoming a widow wasn't one of my goals for today. What are you doing here, apart from following me? I thought you were at the Yard for the day."

My husband grinned. "I was. But now that Lestrade's taken charge of the investigation into Huxley's murder, he thinks it's worth quietly opening up a few lines of inquiry into the death of the first Lady Trent."

"Really? So Lestrade thinks there's something in Mr. Brown's accusations?" I knew Holmes had been inclined to dismiss them. Or so he'd claimed out loud. It was always difficult to judge what Holmes's private opinions might be.

"Huxley's murder is a strange affair," Jack said. "And his secretary Mrs. Clair being killed in an identical way is stranger still."

"At first glance, it looks as though someone is trying to sabotage Sir Galahad's efforts to secure a loan. I don't suppose Mr. Brown could be our killer? We know that he met with Huxley."

"Unfortunately, the medical reports put Mrs. Clair's murder at the exact time that Brown was meeting with Mr. Holmes."

"Which gives him as unimpeachable an alibi as anyone can imagine." I usually mistrusted unimpeachable alibis as a matter of course, but in this case, it was hard to see how Mr. Brown could have been simultaneously in Baker Street and stabbing Mrs. Clair.

"So we're back to either an unknown enemy of Sir Galahad's," Jack said. "Or else—"

"Or else Sir Galahad himself," I finished. "It's possible that while assembling background information for approval of the loan, Mr. Huxley could have stumbled on something to implicate Sir Galahad in his first wife's death. Do we know how she died, by the way?"

"An accident. She apparently fell from one of the castle towers and was killed."

I blinked. "And no one thought to question whether her death was actually accidental or not?"

Jack grimaced. "No one contacted the Yard, at any rate, so the local police must have been satisfied there was nothing suspicious. But that's why I'm here. To stop in at the local police station and ask to see the reports on the incident. And talk to the doctor who signed the death certificate."

I nodded slowly. "Because he ought to be able to tell us whether there were any odd details about the body or the way she fell. And besides, it might have been suicide, mightn't it? And the Trent's family doctor might know about the first Lady Trent's state of mind before she died."

"Right. So I'm here to see"—Jack consulted his notebook—"Dr. Norton, on Clarence Road."

I smiled. Murder was always a grim, ugly, brutal business, and the deaths of Mr. Huxley and Mrs. Clair were no exception. But right now the summer sun was shining, and it wasn't often that I had the chance these days to work on an investigation alongside Jack, with him being so busy at the Yard.

"Perfect," I said. "Because that's exactly where I was going."

***

"It took you longer than usual to realize that you had someone following you," Jack said. "Something on your mind?"

We were walking along Clarence Road, past quaint cottages and more modern town houses, as well as the assortment of tea shops and other stores that had sprung up to cater to the town's recent growth.

"In a way. I was wondering what prompts a man like Sir Galahad Trent to structure his entire life around the pretense that he's one of King Arthur's knights."

"Besides being a few cards short of a full deck, you mean?"

"Well, yes, aside from that. If a man had, say, murdered his wife, do you think the guilt might drive him to want to re-imagine himself as a character from literary fiction? One who lives by a strict code of chivalry and even goes so far as to terrorize any man whom he judges guilty of mistreating the women in his life?"

Jack frowned, considering. "I suppose it's possible. But we can't have it both ways."

"How do you mean?"

"Well, according to what you told me about Mr. Brown's visit to your father this morning, Mr. Brown has accused Sir Galahad of having murdered his first wife and now plotting to kill off his second, Brown's daughter. If Sir Galahad's whole reason for the Round Table charade is that he's tortured by guilt over having killed the first Lady Trent, he'd hardly be planning a duplicate crime, would he?"

"No, I suppose not." I frowned, considering. "What about as a kind of alibi in advance? He creates the persona of a knight in shining armor, chivalrously defending womankind so that when his second wife dies just as his first did, no one will suspect that he could possibly have had anything to do with it?"

"Seems a bit complicated," Jack said. "Besides, there's not a policeman in London who'd actually take the King Arthur act as hard evidence in a murder investigation. He'll still be suspect number one if his new wife does turn up dead."

I sighed. "I suppose you're right. Although Sir Galahad might not necessarily know what suspicious minds policemen have. Anyone who spends his days dressing up like a round table knight doesn't have an entirely firm grip on reality."

"True."

We stopped in front of a tall, prosperous-looking place, built of white stone and surrounded by a low wrought-iron fence. A gold-lettered sign hung over the door, proclaiming, *Godfrey Norton, MD.*

"This is the place," I said. "We'll see if Dr. Norton can offer any insights into either Sir Galahad's character or his wife's death."

A smiling, middle-aged receptionist greeted our entrance to the office. "If you'll just have a seat, the doctor will be with you shortly."

She gestured to a long wooden bench, where a mother and small boy were already waiting.

"Thank you," Jack said. "But I'm actually here with Scotland—"

He broke off. A sharp cry had just sounded from somewhere further inside the office, followed by a shout and a crash of something breaking.

Chapter 12: Becky

"What do you think of Sir Galahad?" Becky asked.

They were on the narrow lane that led away from the castle, through the village and back to the train station.

Flynn shaded his eyes to read the cross-roads sign they were approaching. "You mean do I think he's lost his marbles? Or do I think he's likely to have killed Mr. Huxley?"

Becky shot him a quick look. "So you realized why I was asking him about the dagger?"

"I figured that's what you were thinking. We know what Huxley was stabbed with."

"So?"

"So, do I think Sir Galahad's nutty? Sure, as a fruitcake. Do I think he's a murderer?" Flynn's brows furrowed. "I don't know; it's possible, maybe. But I'm not sure I see it. What motive would he have had?"

Becky had been wondering the same thing, but talking a case out like this was usually the best way to get things clear. So she said, "Maybe Mr. Huxley was going to refuse to grant him the loan he wanted for fixing up the castle?"

Flynn's expression told her he thought that was as flimsy a motive as she did. "Was he going to refuse the loan?"

"Not that I know of," Becky admitted. "According to what Lucy said, I think Huxley was planning to approve it. Besides, even if he had refused, there are other banks and other bankers."

They were coming to the outskirts of the village, and another crossroads. "Huxley's house is this way." She gestured to the sign that read *'Melody Lane.'*

"What about our train?"

Becky consulted her watch. "We've got half an hour until it leaves. Time enough for a quick look around."

* * *

Huxley's house was a solid, three-story brick building with a porch at the front and a conservatory at the back. At the moment, it was dark and quiet-looking, with all the curtains drawn and no sign of anyone about. Becky let out a quick breath of relief. Lucy wouldn't have been angry, even if she had happened to be here and had seen them.

Knowing Lucy, she would have first tried to look stern as she asked for an explanation, then sighed, shaken her head, and finally ended by having to smother a laugh.

But Becky was just as glad not to have to face explaining quite yet.

"We're here," Flynn said. "Now what?"

Becky considered, feeling a sinking in the pit of her stomach, because while it was good news that they'd made it this far undiscovered and without getting into trouble, she also couldn't think of very much they could accomplish just by standing and looking at Huxley's house from the outside.

She was just wondering whether she'd have to admit as much. But then a flicker of movement from around the side of the house caught her eye.

"Look!"

A hooded figure, draped in a dark green cloak, was just emerging from a side door near the glassed-in conservatory.

Becky froze, and beside her, Flynn did the same. But the figure—Becky couldn't even tell for certain whether it was a man or a woman, though from the length of the stride, she thought a man—never glanced back. He cut across the lawn and vanished behind a tall hedgerow.

"Come on!" Becky hissed.

They darted after him, rounding the hedgerow to find that it bordered a narrow, twisting path that led through the woods behind Huxley's house.

Becky looked as far as she could see along the lane. There was no sign of the figure in green, but judging by the position of the sun overhead, she could at least gauge the direction he had taken.

"It looks as though this should lead back to the castle," she said.

The sunlight slanted through the trees overhead, patching the leaf-strewn ground with splotches of gold and shadow. Birds sang from the branches, and a few stray blue and white wildflowers bloomed along the edge of the path.

"We're going to feel like chumps if the fellow we're following is just another of Sir Galahad's cronies, out for a stroll," Flynn said sourly. He was eyeing the surrounding trees and shrubbery with suspicion.

Flynn could clamber across railroad tracks in the face of an oncoming train and navigate the labyrinth-like streets of the worst East-End slums blindfolded. But things like fresh air and flowers and nature always made him uneasy.

"I think I've had just about enough *forsooth's* for one day," he added. "Not to mention I can live without getting cursed by Sir Galahad's magician, whoever he is."

"That's ridiculous. Curses aren't real."

"Know what else isn't real? Any proof that the bloke we're following was actually up to no good."

"Well …" Becky had to admit that was true. She didn't have any concrete reason for thinking that the hooded man had been involved in anything suspicious at Huxley's house. He could be a neighbor, come to pay a condolence call after Huxley's death. "It's just a feeling I have."

"Right." Flynn shot her a look. "So curses aren't real, but you've got the magical ability to tell at a glance when someone's a criminal and needs following. Got it."

Becky started to roll her eyes, then drew in a sharp breath, her attention caught by something on the ground under one of the spreading oak trees just up ahead.

"Flynn—remember the cat that the little girl was chasing? The one we thought might be hurt or ill?"

"Sure. But you heard Sir Galahad. Neither man nor beast shall languish in need of aid and all that. Although how he's going to tell whether a cat's pure of heart—"

Becky interrupted. "Look at that squirrel over there."

She pointed to the small furry brown creature that was stumbling around at the foot of the tree. It would take a few staggering steps, try to scramble up the tree trunk, then fall back, collapsing onto the ground.

Flynn frowned, his skeptical look immediately vanishing. "You're right, it's acting a lot like that cat did."

Becky crept forward, approaching the squirrel, which had collapsed onto the mossy ground and was now lying on its side, panting. "Come here, it's all right," she murmured. "I'm not going to hurt you."

The creature didn't resist when she picked it up.

"What's wrong with it?" Flynn asked.

"How would I know that?"

"You're the one who's always reading Dr. Watson's old medical textbooks."

"Believe it or not, they don't cover common squirrel ailments." Becky took out her handkerchief from her pocket so that she could wrap it around the small creature. It scrabbled only briefly, then lay quiet, still panting on the palms of her cupped hands.

"Maybe it got into poison?" Flynn suggested. "Some people leave out poisoned meat or milk to try and kill rats."

Becky could feel the hectic drumming of the squirrel's heartbeat through the handkerchief. It seemed fast, although she had no idea what the normal resting heart rate for a squirrel was. "If someone around here left poison out, I suppose both the squirrel and the cat could have gotten into it. Although I haven't heard of any poison that would make an animal act this way. Usually people trying to get rid of rats use arsenic or something else that kills quickly."

There was always Flynn's theory about drunkenness. Holding the squirrel's paws through the handkerchief so that she wouldn't get scratched, Becky bent her head and sniffed at the small animal's nose and mouth. But she couldn't detect any odor of spirits or other alcohol.

A soft *crack* sounded from somewhere in the woods behind them, like a small twig breaking. Becky lifted her head, listening. "Do you think someone's following us?" she murmured.

Flynn shrugged. "Could be another squirrel. Or someone out for a walk. Lots of people probably use this path."

That was true, but Becky couldn't entirely erase the unpleasant prickling feeling that slid from the top of her spine all the way down towards her toes.

"We'd better keep going," she said. "Whoever the man in the cloak is, he must be way ahead of us by now."

She tucked the squirrel into the pocket of her skirt and led the way, keeping her ears pricked for any more sounds from behind. None came, but after they'd gone a few hundred yards more, she sniffed.

"Do you smell that?"

Flynn breathed in, sampling the air. "Smells like … smoke? But maybe it's just from someone's chimney."

"In the middle of July? No one's lighting fires on a day like today."

The waft of smoke was mixed with an odd, herb-y smell. Not unpleasant, but both sharp and sweet at the same time.

Becky grabbed Flynn's arm. "Look there!"

Scanning the trees all around them, she'd spotted a patch of gray stonework just visible through the screen of leaves and branches. Her uneasiness must be catching, because Flynn didn't point out that it could be anything, from a simple crofter's cottage to an ancient stone wall that had once bordered a now-abandoned field.

Instead, he nodded and crept forwards with her. They made their way quietly through the trees, bending branches aside, both of them placing their feet carefully to avoid making too much noise. The structure that was finally revealed was a small stone hut with a thatched roof and windows covered by rough wooden shutters.

They stopped, drawing back behind the trunk of a tall tree so that they could peer out cautiously at the hut and the small clearing in which it stood.

There were no signs of life and no smoke coming from the chimney, but the herb-laced smell of burning was stronger here. Definitely coming from somewhere nearby.

"Where exactly are we, do you think?" Flynn whispered.

Becky frowned, trying to calculate. "Somewhere near the castle, I'm fairly sure. Listen. You can just hear the music from the carousel."

"So what now? Do we try to get a look inside?" Flynn nodded towards the hut.

Peeking inside would be difficult. The place might look ramshackle, but Becky could see how tightly the shutters fit over the windows, with not even a chink appearing between the wooden slats and the stonework.

"Let's have a look all around first, just to make sure there's no one about," she finally said. "You go right, I'll go left, and we'll meet up at the back."

Flynn nodded and set off, slipping quietly around the perimeter of the clearing, keeping inside the tree line. Becky did the same, moving in the opposite direction and trying to ignore the uneasiness that was still slithering like a nest of snakes inside her gut.

All of this was probably nothing but her imagination. The hooded figure they'd followed was just a local neighbor, this cottage was where he lived, and—

The squirrel had been riding compliantly in Becky's pocket until this, but now it suddenly startled and started scrabbling frantically, hooking its claws in the fabric of Becky's skirt.

She put her hand down, trying to quiet it. "Shhh, it's all—"

A footstep sounded behind her, but before she could turn, arms seized her, and a pad of something sweet and sickly smelling was clamped over her face. Becky struggled, kicking, trying to stamp on her attacker's foot or elbow him in the stomach, but the grip didn't relax.

Her head spun, her vision darkening. Then everything stopped.

Chapter 13: Lucy

Jack reacted instantly, vaulting over the receptionist's desk and pushing through the swinging door labeled *Surgery*. I ran after him down the short hallway and into a white, clinical examination room. A stout, balding man lay on the floor amid a shower of broken glass and splintered wood.

The window, too, was shattered, the light curtains that had covered it now flapping in the breeze.

Jack gave a quick glance back at me.

I nodded. "Go! I'll stay with him."

In an instant, Jack had gone out through the broken window, landing in the street outside. Despite what I'd said, my nerves still tensed with the urge to follow after him. Watching him run towards danger was something I'd grown accustomed to, but at the same time it never got any easier.

Jack could run faster than I could, though. My presence would only slow him down, and besides, the man on the floor was hurt.

I knelt beside him. "Doctor Norton?"

The doctor had only been stunned rather than knocked fully unconscious. An angry red mark that would no doubt turn into a nasty bruise showed on his forehead. But at the sound of my voice, he blinked, peering dazedly up at me.

"What—who—" he started struggling to sit up.

"Try to lie still until we know how badly you're injured," I told him. "Can you tell me what happened?"

Dr. Norton sank back, briefly shutting his eyes. "I … I heard a sound. In the back room, where I keep my records." He gestured feebly towards a door at the rear of the examination room. "I went to investigate. There was a man. He struck me. I fell backwards. Knocked over the shelf where I keep medicines on hand." He nodded towards the glass and wood on the floor.

"This man. Did you recognize him?"

"No. But he wore a mask. I never saw his face." He passed a hand across his eyes. "I must … we ought to summon the police."

"No need," I said. I glanced at the window. There was no sign of Jack yet, but then he'd only just left. "My husband—the man who just went after the intruder—is a sergeant with Scotland Yard. He'll take your statement."

Assuming that he came back, that was.

The door opened behind us, and the motherly looking receptionist put her head in. "Are you all right, Dr.—oh!" she broke off with a gasp at the sight of Dr. Norton and the broken window.

"It's all right," I told her. "But would you tell Dr. Norton's patients that they'll have to come back another day? And then maybe bring a cup of tea for the doctor?"

***

Five minutes later, Dr. Norton stared at me across his rapidly cooling mug of tea. He was a small man, with a rotund frame and a high, domed forehead and a fringe of white hair around his ears.

He looked intelligent, and was probably an excellent doctor. But at the moment, he had the bewildered look of an ordinary citizen who's suddenly been forced into a headlong meeting with unexpected, intentional violence.

Most people lived their lives in peace, without ever facing an intruder bent on doing them physical harm. The simple shock of such an assault was often as stunning and painful as the injuries themselves.

"I feel as though I'm being terribly unhelpful," Dr. Norton said. He had fixed a large square of sticking plaster over the bruise on his head, and beneath it, his gaze was both dazed and troubled. "But I can tell you so little. It all happened so quickly."

"That's all right," I told him. My own nerves were twitching with awareness that Jack still hadn't returned. But right now, Dr. Norton needed calm. "Just tell me everything that you can remember."

Dr. Norton took a swallow of his tea. "Very well. I had just finished with a patient, and was sitting at my desk, making notes in the patient's file before asking Mrs. Rudge to send the next one in. That was when I heard a noise in the small back room where I keep the cabinets that contain all my patient files."

"Just your current patients? Or past ones, also?" I asked.

"Oh, past ones, as well," Dr. Norton said. "Some of the files date back to the earliest days of my practice here, which was nearly thirty years ago."

"Do you have any idea how someone could have gotten in?" I asked.

"I suppose through the window. I always keep it locked, but there are no bars. We have never had reason, here, to worry overmuch about burglars, you see." Dr. Norton took another sip of his tea. "But I knew that no one should be back there, so I went to investigate. I opened the door—" his voice faltered briefly.

"This is where things happened at such a speed that I scarcely know how to give you a clear account. I saw a man bending over one of the file drawers, which he had pulled out and appeared to be rummaging through. But I caught only a brief glimpse of him. The moment he heard me in the doorway, he spun and sprang at me. He struck me with some sort of weapon that he had in one hand. A small, blunt affair."

The doctor reached gingerly up to touch the bandage on his forehead.

"A cosh?"

"Is that the name of such a device? I'm afraid I wouldn't know. He struck me, and I fell back. Then I stumbled—or perhaps he pushed me?—into the set of shelves where I keep all ready-made medicines that I have on hand here. I fell. I believe I lost consciousness for a moment or two, though I think I can just recall hearing the window breaking, which I suppose must have been how he made his escape. The next thing I can clearly remember is your bending over me."

"The man who attacked you," I said. "Can you tell us anything about him? I know you say he wore a mask. But what kind of mask, for a start?"

"The mask?" Dr. Norton's brow crinkled in an effort of remembrance. "It was a green velvet affair. Now that I come to think of it, it reminded me of the illustrations in a book of stories of Robin Hood that I had as a boy." He smiled faintly. "You know, the tale in which Robin Hood enters the archery contest in disguise, under the Sheriff of Nottingham's nose."

That couldn't be mere coincidence. Although it looked as though either our intruder or Dr. Norton was mixing up his fairy tales.

I wished more than ever that Jack were present to hear this. But I said, "Is there anything else you can say about the intruder? His height or build, for example?"

"Really, I don't know." Dr. Norton shook his head in frustration. "He was ... average height, I think. Perhaps a little taller? And neither fat nor thin that I can recall. But as I say, I saw him for only a second or two."

"Can you remember what he was wearing?"

"I don't ..." Dr. Norton screwed his eyes shut, still frowning, then opened them again. "Why, of course. I'm afraid I'm being very stupid. I have diagnosed many patients with shock, but have never experienced the phenomenon myself. I must say, I am finding it entirely unpleasant." Another brief flicker of humor showed in the doctor's gaze, then he said, "But I remember now, the man was wearing a kind of cloak—the old-fashioned type, made of some dark material. That, coupled with the mask, must have been what put Robin Hood and the Sheriff of Nottingham into my mind."

"I see. Thank you," I added. I studied Dr. Norton, debating whether he looked fit enough to go into the back room and try to determine which files had been opened. Or whether I should wait for Jack.

How long had he been gone, now? A quarter of an hour? Twenty minutes?

Having something concrete to do was always better than any of the nightmare images that came crowding in at times like these, so I stood up.

"Do you think—" I began.

Jack appeared in the frame of the broken window. Alive, but with his entire right hand and arm dripping blood.

CHAPTER 14: FLYNN

Flynn came awake in stages. First, he had the murky feeling that something was wrong. Then he started to be aware of a throbbing pain in his skull. Then finally his eyes snapped open and he sat up with a jolt as his memories came back.

He was in what looked like some kind of a cellar. The floor was hard-packed dirt, and the walls were made of damp stone that was starting to crumble in spots. Light filtered through chinks in the wooden trapdoor that was directly over his head. The door was a good ten feet up, far too high for him to reach. But at least the sunlight was bright and enough not just to let him see but to tell him that he hadn't been unconscious for very long.

He stood up and looked around, realizing for the first time that he wasn't alone. Becky was lying a few feet away behind him. Before he had a chance to worry about whether she was all right, her eyes opened, and she sat up, too.

"What happened?"

"I got slugged on the head." Flynn felt the knot on the back of his skull and winced. "Is that how they got you?"

Becky shook her head. "Chloroform. At least, that's what it smelled like." She looked around the cellar, too. "Do you think this is Sir Galahad's dungeon?"

"Doesn't seem likely. If it was the dungeon, we wouldn't be

able to see sunlight." Flynn pointed to the trapdoor. "Aren't dungeons always down below the castle?"

"True. Probably." Becky eyed the trap door, gauging the distance between it and them. "Too high to jump, but maybe we can find a way to climb up and reach it."

"Maybe. But unless whoever tossed us down here is stupid, it'll be locked from the outside."

Becky blew out a breath of frustration. She always hated being stuck with a problem that couldn't be tackled head-on. "We can at least look around and see whether there's anything to climb on."

Flynn was tempted to say that as far as he could see, whoever had stocked this cellar had forgotten to throw down a ladder or two. But instead he shrugged, turned, and started to edge his way towards the nearest wall, squinting so that his eyes would adjust to the dark.

Maybe they'd find something to help. And having something to do—even if it got them nowhere in the end—was better than just sitting still and wondering who'd tossed them down there and whether they were planning to come back. He was trying to ignore it, but his chest felt tight and his skin felt hot and itchy, the way it always did when he was trapped inside four closed-in walls. Even in Mr. Holmes's rooms in Baker Street, he was a lot happier when Mr. Holmes left a window open.

His foot connected with something on the earthen ground, and bending over, Flynn felt the smooth, cool surface of something glass. He stooped and picked up a couple of glass bottles.

"What is it?" Becky asked.

Flynn examined the labels on the bottles. "Lemonade. Probably the same stuff they sell up at the fair."

"Is it safe to drink, do you suppose?"

Flynn felt the caps on the bottles. "Seems like they're still sealed."

There was just enough light for him to make out Becky's frown. "Still, if we're dealing with a poisoner—oh!" She broke off with a sharp gasp and felt for her pocket, then let out a breath of relief. "I'd completely forgotten about the squirrel we picked up. But he's still here." She took the small animal out and held it on the palm of her hand. "And he seems all right—I think he's maybe a little bit better, even."

If Flynn had been the one to choose today's good news bulletin, he would have picked something other than a squirrel looking healthier. But he supposed beggars didn't get to argue about details.

"So whatever he got into wasn't fatal?"

"It doesn't look like it." Becky touched the squirrel's head with the tip of one finger. It shook itself, jumped down off her hand, twitched its tail, and then scampered to the corner of the cellar, where it sat up on its haunches and started making irritated-sounding chattering noises.

"Yeah, me too, mate," Flynn said. "But until we figure a way out of here, it looks like you're stuck with us."

"Did you find anything besides the lemonade?" Becky asked.

"Didn't see anything, but I didn't really have a chance to look."

The cellar wasn't large, but with the only light coming in through the trapdoor, the edges of the room were nearly pitch black. They split up again, starting towards opposite corners.

The trapdoor rattled as though a bolt was being drawn back, then lifted aside.

Flynn jumped and heard Becky gasp from the other side of

the room. Both of them looked up in time to see a face appear in the sunlit gap above them. A woman's face, crowned by a mass of red hair.

Flynn's jaw dropped. Whoever he'd been expecting, it wasn't the woman from the train station, the one with the ice cream who'd accidentally bumped into Becky.

What was even more surprising, though, was that the woman looked just as shocked to see them as Flynn was to see her.

"Good heavens." Her voice was different, somehow. Less fluttery, and with an accent that reminded Flynn of Lucy. "How did you get down there?" Then, before either of them could answer, she gave a half-laugh. "I suppose you think that a strange question. You're probably assuming that I'm the one who trapped you down there. And I realize that my word will mean nothing to you at all, but I do give you my solemn promise that it wasn't in fact me."

Becky got her voice back, folding her arms across her chest. "Wonderful," she said flatly. "So you'll be able to toss a rope down here and help get us out, then."

Her tone of voice made it clear that she didn't expect the red-haired woman to do anything of the kind. Flynn hadn't really been expecting it, either. And yet the strange thing was, he would have sworn that a look of genuine regret passed across the woman's face.

"I'm sorry. That's just what I can't do. You see, I simply can't let anyone in this neighborhood even begin to suspect that I was here and found you. If only I hadn't called on—" she seemed to catch herself and gave a quick shake of her head. "Never mind. But the stakes are much higher than either of you know, and I've got to avoid arousing anyone's suspicions at all cost. But

I promise to send help to you as soon as I possibly can. That much I can do."

She started to close the trapdoor hatch again, but then stopped. "Oh—wait a moment. Here." She reached into the handbag she was carrying, fumbled a moment, then tossed a brown paper-wrapped parcel of something down to land on the ground at Becky's feet. "You don't have any reason to believe me on this score, either, but I would strongly advise against eating or drinking anything left with you down there. But everything I've just given you is perfectly safe."

"Let me guess, you promise?" Flynn said, raising an eyebrow.

The red-haired woman actually smiled at that, a dimple appearing on one side of her mouth. "I'm truly sorry to leave you both. But unless I'm underestimating your resourcefulness, you very likely won't even be here by the time I can send help."

CHAPTER 15: LUCY

"This is quite nasty," Dr. Norton said. He was examining the long slash that ran up the inner side of Jack's arm, and he spoke with professional calm, sounding steadier than I'd yet heard him since our arrival.

I wasn't the only one to benefit from having a concrete job to do.

"Yes, well done," I said. I wasn't usually squeamish about the sight of blood, but I kept having to avert my gaze as Dr. Norton swabbed the cut and got ready to apply sutures. "What happened?"

Jack grimaced. "I got careless. I saw the man outside, scrambling over the back wall"—he nodded towards the bricked-in courtyard visible through the windows—"so I chased him. Must have gone almost a mile, round about town. Whoever he is, we know one thing about him: he knows this area well."

"Did you see his face?" I asked.

"Never. He mostly had his back to me, and he was wearing some kind of mask."

Dr. Norton was applying some sort of antiseptic to Jack's cut. I knew from personal experience that it had to sting, but Jack didn't move or wince.

"I lost sight of him when he went round a corner, so I sped up, trying not to let him get away. Instead, he sprang out at me from a doorway. That's when this happened." Jack nodded at the gash on his arm.

"It looks like a knife cut—or even a sword," Dr. Norton said.

"Something like that," Jack said. "He had a dagger. An old-fashioned kind of affair with a jeweled hilt. He got in this cut, but then I kicked the knife out of his hand. I would have tackled him. But a girl came out of her house just then. We were in an alleyway behind a row of town homes, and this girl had come out to empty the trash can. Eleven or twelve years old. She never even saw us until she was already outside her door. But the fellow in the mask grabbed her right away. Pulled out a gun and held it to her head."

"He had a knife *and* a gun?" I asked.

Our nameless intruder had been remarkably well-armed, considering his objective had been a simple act of burglary on an elderly doctor who so far as we knew hadn't a single weapon with which to fight back.

"A Remington five shot pocket revolver," Jack said. "Looked like a .32 caliber."

I wasn't surprised that he'd noted the make and model of the gun. If only he'd had more time or gotten closer, he probably could have told us the serial number of the weapon, as well.

Dr. Norton snipped a length from a spool of surgical thread and started to stitch up the wound in Jack's arm. Jack kept speaking without even seeming to notice.

"He didn't say anything, but he still made it clear he was going to shoot her if I tried to stop him or come any closer. So I backed off. Left the knife on the ground and didn't move."

Jack's voice was tight with an echo of the frustration he must have felt in the moment.

"What happened?"

"He made it all the way to the end of the alley, dragging the girl with him. Then he gave her a shove and ran off. I couldn't go after him. He'd got too much of a head start, for one thing, and the girl was crying and terrified out of her wits for another. I had to pick her up and help her get back home."

"You couldn't have done anything else," I agreed.

I could see that Jack knew that, too. But he didn't like it any more than I would have done in his place.

"I was just about to ask Dr. Norton to look through his records," I said. "Maybe once he's finished with your stitches, we can find out whether the intruder took anything and what he might have been after."

Chapter 16: Lucy

Dr. Norton stepped carefully through the scattered papers in his back room.

Wooden file cabinets lined the walls on three sides, but it looked as though only one of the cabinet drawers had been wrenched open. The drawer lay overturned on the floor, with the manilla folders spilling out all around.

Jack and I remained in the doorway so as not to disturb any evidence or add to the confusion.

"How does your arm feel?" I asked in an undertone.

"Hurts." Jack shrugged, then gave me a quick flash of a reassuring smile. "I'm all right. And just think how thrilled Becky will be to have a patient to doctor right in our own home. She'll probably insist on changing the bandages every half hour, just so she can get more practice in."

"Probably."

A brief flicker of uneasiness went through me, though, at the mention of Becky. I'd had to leave her at home alone today, and that almost never ended well.

Dr. Norton looked up, holding an armful of files and paperwork. "It appears to me that only one file is missing," he said. "That of Lady Rose Trent. Sir Roderick—excuse me, I should say Sir Galahad's late wife."

I let out a breath. Somewhere in the back of my mind, I had been expecting that. Coincidences occasionally happened, but someone breaking into Dr. Norton's files today of all days was simply too big of a one to be believed.

"You're certain?" Jack asked.

"Yes, yes, quite sure. Here is the file in which her records were contained, you see." Dr. Norton held up the manilla folder so that we could see the label on the tab: *Lady Rose Trent*. "But it is empty. My notes are all gone, nor are they among any of these papers that remain."

Dr. Norton gestured to the few remaining records that still lay on the floor. Then he set the empty file on top of one of the other cabinets and studied both Jack and me in turn.

The shock of the attack and the injury he'd taken had worn off by now, and his gaze was keen. "It would appear that the name of Lady Trent is not unknown to you," he said. "Which leads me to conclude that there is a particular and not unrelated reason that a police sergeant from Scotland Yard happened to visit my surgery this afternoon."

Jack and I exchanged another brief glance, and I nodded.

"You're quite right, sir," Jack said. "I understand you're bound by the rules of patient confidentiality. But I must tell you that I came here authorized to make inquiries into the death of the first Lady Trent."

Dr. Norton's gaze narrowed slightly, and he once again scrutinized Jack's face. He appeared to like what he saw, because after a moment he nodded and seemed to make up his mind.

"Strictly speaking, my patient is dead, which means that I am no longer bound to keep her secrets. Or rather, it means that

I have a higher duty to the pursuit of justice. This inquiry into Lady Trent's death: am I right in imagining that Scotland Yard is viewing it as a murder investigation?"

"You don't sound surprised by that," Jack said.

Dr. Norton sighed heavily, rubbing a hand up and down his face. "No. No, may Heaven forgive me, I cannot say that I am shocked by what you say. Not," he added quickly, "that I had evidence that her death was anything but a tragic accident. If I had done, I should of course have reported it to the authorities. As it was, I was asked by the coroner for my opinion, and was forced to say that the fatal injuries observed on the body of Lady Trent were in every way consistent with an accidental fall."

"No defensive wounds?" Jack asked. "No bruises on her wrists or upper arms?"

Those were the sorts of injuries you would expect to see if she had been pushed from the castle tower. But Dr. Norton gave a decided shake of his head. "No, nothing of that kind whatsoever. And I did look for those sorts of marks most particularly. Not only were there no bruises, scrapes, or other injuries that were not consistent with her fall, we had the eyewitness evidence of no less than six of the household servants that she was entirely alone on the top of the tower when the accident occurred."

"Six?"

Dr. Norton sighed again. "Indeed. Lord and Lady Trent were alone at home that day, save for the servants. There were no visitors. Sir Galahad was outside in the garden, conversing with a friend of his who lives in a cottage on the estate."

"The friend's name?" Jack asked.

"His name is Calloway—Peter Calloway, I believe. Although Sir Galahad calls him Merlin."

My eyebrows went up. "Of course he does."

I should probably have expected that there would be a Merlin somewhere in the picture.

Dr. Norton's expression was wry. "Yes. Mr. Calloway was an old school friend of Sir Galahad's, I believe. They met at university, where Mr. Calloway was doing research into medieval history. Sir Galahad invited him down here, to live in a private cottage and be free to continue his research. At any rate, on the morning of Lady Trent's death, they were together in the garden, discussing plans for some new herbal beds. Both the head gardener and the under gardener saw them there—and not only saw them, but were actually speaking to them at the time Lady Trent fell from the tower. Sir Galahad was giving them instructions on how the new garden beds were to be laid out when they heard Lady Trent's scream. They all ran together—Sir Galahad, Mr. Calloway, and the gardeners—and were the first to discover Lady Trent's body."

Which certainly seemed to eliminate both Sir Galahad and Merlin as suspects.

"And the other witnesses?" Jack asked.

Dr. Norton started to tick them off on his fingers. "The housekeeper passed Lady Trent on the stairs. She wanted to consult with Lady Trent about the menu for a dinner party that the Trents were giving on the following day. But she said later that Lady Trent did not wish to speak of it then, and simply brushed past her with scarcely a word."

"Did the housekeeper think she seemed upset?" I asked.

Dr. Norton pursed his lips. "She did not use the words agitated or upset in the account she gave later. She thought Lady Trent was preoccupied, certainly. But then, Lady Trent tended to be a passionate, highly emotional woman. The household staff had become quite accustomed to putting up with moodiness and occasional fits of temper from her. To continue, the housekeeper saw Lady Trent ascending the staircase in the downstairs hallway to the second floor. Once upstairs, she encountered two of the housemaids who were dusting the bedrooms and laying fresh fires in the grates. Neither of them spoke to Lady Trent, but they saw her going to the door of the stairwell that led up to the tower, and both could swear that she was alone."

That made five servants so far. "And the last witness?" I asked.

"The last witness was the boy whose job it is to clean the household knives and boots. He had overslept, and thus failed to return Sir Galahad's freshly cleaned boots to the wardrobe first thing in the morning. So with Sir Galahad out of the house, he had seized the opportunity to remedy his error, and had crept up to Sir Galahad's room. I should explain," Dr. Norton added, "that Sir Galahad's bedroom is almost directly beneath the tower."

"I see. So the knives and boots boy saw Lady Trent?"

"No, he didn't actually see her ascending into the tower. But while he was engaged in placing the boots in Sir Galahad's wardrobe, he heard a scream. I imagine it gave him quite a nasty start. But though not an early riser, young Jerry is a bright lad, alert and fast on his feet. He realized at once where the scream had come from, and went running up the tower stairs. Lady Trent had already gone over the side of the parapet by the time he got there. He looked over the edge and saw her body down below. But he was also able to swear that the top of the tower was quite empty. He can have arrived only a bare handful of seconds after Lady Trent fell, but there was no one with her up on the tower, nor did he meet anyone on the stairs."

"That seems to let out murder as a possibility," Jack said. "And yet you must have had a reason for going into everything so carefully, tracking down the witnesses' accounts and ruling out the possibility that someone—particularly Sir Galahad himself—could have been involved?"

Dr. Norton rubbed the space between his eyes, looking unhappy. "Yes. We now come to the part of the story where I cannot help but feel that I might have done more. And yet, even now, I am at a loss to know what exactly I could have accomplished, if I had ... well, but you must judge for yourselves." He was silent a moment, seeming to collect his thoughts, and then said, "To begin, I'm not sure whether you know of Lady Rose Trent's background?"

"Very little," I said. "Only that she was also an American, like the current Lady Trent?"

"Indeed. I had never, of course, met her before her and Sir Galahad's marriage. But from my very earliest encounters with them as a couple, I formed the impression that the marriage had been an unfortunate one."

"From her perspective or from his?" I asked.

"From hers, largely. Sir Galahad—well, as I say, I have had my practice here for thirty-odd years, which means that I have known him since he was a boy. I treated him for mumps when he was a child. He has always been"—Dr. Norton seemed to search for words—"something of a dreamer, rather than a man of practicalities. He and reality have very little to do with one another, except as it relates to his grand passion, the running of his estate and castle. And so I do not think that he was in any very great way dissatisfied with his American wife. He was practical enough to have sought out a woman whose dowry could provide the money he needed to restore the castle, and he found that in Rose. She was also extremely pretty, intelligent, and could be charming when she so chose. For Lady Trent, though—" Dr. Norton broke off and shook his head. "I do not believe that the marriage was so much her own choosing as that of her family. They wanted the prestige of the title and the old family name that Sir Galahad could provide."

And had been willing to sell their daughter in order to obtain them. London society was full of those American dollar duchesses, as the term went, and I had gone to school with girls like Rose Trent back in the States: girls whose mothers had raised them to believe that their highest calling was to snare a husband from the British aristocracy.

"Lady Trent and Sir Galahad were from the first ill-suited to one another. They were nothing alike in their temperaments and shared no common interests. Rose had no interest whatsoever in Sir Galahad's pet project of restoring the castle," Dr. Norton went on. "She proclaimed it gloomy and dull and was continually pestering him to buy a town house in London, where they could live in modern comfort and attend grand society affairs."

"How did Sir Galahad take all of that?" I asked.

"The same way he always takes anything unpleasant, or any aspect of life that does not fit in with his happy dream of Arthurian romance—by simply ignoring it. I do not mean to suggest that he was cruel to his wife, far from it. He simply could not comprehend how anyone could fail to be less than enamored with his castle and his playacting, and thus all of his wife's complaints and protests passed in one ear and out the other, so to speak." Dr. Norton paused. "Most of this, I may add, was known to me because it was common knowledge among our community here. Lord and Lady Trent were, by nature of their position and eminence, the subject of considerable local gossip. My own particular knowledge, if I may term it so, came about when Lady Trent decided to consult me in my capacity as a medical professional."

"Was she ill?" Jack asked.

The doctor pursed his lips again. "I did not think so at the time. My opinion after our initial appointment was that she was simply lonely and bored, and had sought out medical care as a way of passing the time. And perhaps with the hope of revenging herself on her husband, as well, for his attitude of vague, kindly indifference to her unhappiness. I had the impression that she was hoping I would diagnose her with some disease or nervous complain that would require her to leave the area and the castle for medical reasons." A brief flicker of humor gathered about the corners of Dr. Norton's eyes. "In the same way that doctors sometimes order their patients to the seaside in hopes that they will benefit from the milder climate and cleaner air, I think that Rose Trent was wishing for a prescription that included London, the theater, and the opera."

"I take it you couldn't oblige?" I asked.

"No. Her actual complaint—at least, the reason she gave for her initial visit to me—was that she was having difficulty sleeping. She also spoke of unsettling nightmares when she did manage to drop off. She was quite indefinite about it all, and as I say, I formed the impression that her visit to me was made largely in hope of strengthening her case that she and Sir Galahad ought to leave the castle. I prescribed her a mild sleeping draught, and frankly did not expect to see her again."

"But you did?" Jack said.

"Yes. About a month later, Lady Trent came again. Her nightmares had grown worse, she said—so much so that she was afraid of going to sleep. On this visit, I had to revise my initial opinion that the greatest ailment with which she was suffering was mere boredom. There was still nothing physically wrong with her that I could identify, and yet she appeared to me to be in a genuine state of nervous agitation. She had lost weight and was strained and tense, as though something were preying on her mind. This time, I gave it as my opinion that perhaps she might benefit from taking a rest cure at one of the health spas that specialize in the treatment of nervous exhaustion: Bath or Tunbridge Wells or even Malvern, if she wished to try hydrotherapy. To my very great surprise, she refused utterly to even consider the idea."

I frowned. "She refused?"

"She said that she was very happy here, and had no wish to leave the neighborhood or her home at the castle. What could I do?" Dr. Norton raised his hand and let it fall. "I could hardly force her, and as I say, her ailment seemed to me to be entirely of a nervous rather than a physical disposition. I did not see that any good could come of trying to persuade her into a course of action to which she was, for whatever reason, violently opposed."

"Do you have any idea why she was so opposed?" Jack asked. "According to everything you've said, the idea of leaving Tottenham and the castle ought to have been exactly what she wanted."

"I'm afraid I have no answer to that," Dr. Norton said. "Nor did I ever discover what had led to her sudden change of heart. I saw her only once more. But her final visit to me was without question the most disturbing." He paused, looking down at the empty file in his hands. "Lady Trent arrived at my office here quite distraught. Not on account of her own health—at least, not that she mentioned. She said that her distress was due to the death of her pet dog, a Pekinese that she had possessed since the days before her marriage and thus had brought with her when she came to live at the castle. The animal had suddenly taken sick and died the day before she saw me, and she claimed that she had the gravest suspicions that her husband had poisoned it."

I looked at the doctor in surprise. Jack's expression showed that he too was plainly taken aback by the accusation.

"She thought Sir Galahad had deliberately poisoned the animal?"

"So she said." Dr. Norton rubbed his nose with the back of his thumb, looking troubled. "It was not a claim that I took seriously, despite Lady Trent's obvious distress. As I mentioned before, I have known Sir Galahad since he was a child, and the idea that he would cold-bloodedly administer poison to a beloved house pet was—*is*—absolutely contrary to everything I know of his character."

"What reason did Lady Trent give for her suspicions?" I asked.

"That was just it. She could give none—nothing concrete, only tears and wild accusations. She claimed that Sir Galahad must have been jealous of her affection for the dog, and had poisoned the creature out of spite. But that, again, ran contrary to everything I knew of Sir Galahad. Dreamy, vague, and idealistic he may be. But I would not say that he has a spiteful or a jealous bone in his body. Nor, I might add, could even Lady Trent—despite the certainty of her accusations—offer me a single actual example of a time when Sir Galahad had expressed any ill-feeling or dislike of the animal."

"Yet she definitely believed that her husband had killed the dog?" I asked.

"She did. She said she did. And yet—" Dr. Norton paused, his brow furrowed, plainly searching for words. "It's difficult to explain the feeling I had. The nearest I can come is to say that I felt not as though she necessarily believed her husband to be guilty, but as though she wanted to believe him guilty. As though in speaking of it, she sought to convince not only me, but also herself."

"Almost as though there were someone else she suspected, but didn't want to believe guilty?" Jack suggested.

"As to that, I cannot say. She gave me no other names. And after securing from me a second prescription for a sleeping draught, she left, in what seemed outwardly at least to be a calmer frame of mind. But then—"

Dr. Norton stopped and fell silent.

"But then Lady Trent died?" I finished.

"Yes," Dr. Norton agreed heavily. "Then Lady Trent died, and under circumstances that, if not overtly suspicious, were certainly both dramatic and strange. And yet in light of the evidence, I cannot see—even now, I cannot see—how her husband or anyone else for that matter can have been in any way culpable in her death. Except perhaps in a strictly moral sense. It has been in my mind since her death that perhaps Sir Galahad's neglect of her unhappiness caused her to become unbalanced—unbalanced enough to take her own life."

"Do you think Lady Trent is the kind of woman likely to have committed suicide?" Jack asked.

"I should not have thought it of her. She seemed to me—even agitated and upset as she was during her appointments with me—to have far too healthy a regard for her own importance to wish to destroy herself. But how can I say for certain?" Dr. Norton gave a helpless shrug. "I met with her on only those three occasions; it is not as though I can claim to have known her well. I confess I had put the matter out of my mind as one of those question marks we doctors must simply learn to live with in the course of our careers, and was content to let poor Lady Rose rest as quietly as possible in her grave. Until today."

"Do you know Mr. Huxley?" I asked. "He worked at Tottenham Bank."

"Huxley?" Dr. Norton's brows drew together, but he gave no sign of recognition—or of having heard of Mr. Huxley's murder. Of course, it wouldn't have made it into the papers yet. "Huxley, no, I don't think I know anyone by that name. He certainly wasn't a patient of mine."

The doctor stopped and divided a searching glance between Jack and myself. "I take it that your presence here—and the break-in to purloin Lady Trent's file—means that new evidence has come to light in the matter of her death?"

"I'm sure you'll understand why we can't share details at this time," Jack said. He smiled to soften the words. "Though we're grateful for all you've told us."

"Of course—of course. Anything I can do," Dr. Norton said. "As I have said, my conscience has never been entirely easy on the matter. I welcome the chance to at least partly rectify any negligence there may have been on my part." He cast a quick and slightly nervous glance around at the partially restored order of his records room, and added, in a different tone, "Do you imagine that the intruder will be back?"

"I wouldn't think so," Jack said. "My guess is that they found what they were after the first time, and won't risk getting caught by returning. But if it would make you feel safer, you could telephone to the local police station and ask them to put a constable on guard here for tonight. I can speak to whoever's in charge for you."

"Yes, yes, thank you." Dr. Norton looked relieved. "I shall do that."

"Would you mind letting me use your telephone afterwards?" I asked. At Jack's questioning look, I said, "I'd like to ring Holmes. We should let him know that we'll be returning to London later than we'd expected. And I want to ask whether there have been any developments on his end."

CHAPTER 17: BECKY

"Is it me, or does this day just keep getting stranger?" Flynn asked, when the trapdoor had shut and they'd heard the rattle of the bolt being shot back into place.

"I know." Fear and anger were currently having a fight inside Becky's chest, but she was hoping that anger would win. That was always better than being afraid. "That was the same woman—"

Who was pretending to conduct a census survey, was what she said. But the words collided in mid-air with Flynn's, *From the train station.*

"What?"

"What?"

Their *what's* collided in mid-air, too. Becky took a breath and started over. "What are you talking about? What woman from the train station?"

"The one who was walking just ahead of us when we got off the train. There was a man with her. Didn't get a good look at his face, but he was dressed like he owns stock in a laundry soap company—you know, all white flannel. Then I saw her again on her own up at the fair. She was the one who bumped into you and almost dropped her ice cream."

"*What?*" Becky stared at him. Then she squeezed her eyes shut, trying to remember. "I never really got a good look at her face," she said. Her hands bunched into fists in frustration. "She had that parasol, and I wasn't really paying proper attention."

She could imagine what Mr. Holmes would say about that. But there was no help for it now.

"But the woman who just left us, she was the same one who came to the door at home this morning, I'm certain of it. Her hair is different. The red hair must be a wig, because her hair was dark this morning, and I'm almost sure it was natural. But I know it was her."

They were silent for a beat or two. Becky didn't know what Flynn was thinking, but for her, the reality of their situation was fully sinking in. She'd been dazed by the chloroform at first, and then distracted by the red-haired woman's arrival. But now she was growing aware that they were stuck down here, alone in the dark, and that no one knew where they were. She hadn't even left word of any kind for Lucy or Jack that she and Flynn had gone to Tottenham this afternoon.

"Well, on the bright side," Flynn finally said, "we've got proof positive now that this woman, whoever she may be, is somehow mixed up with Sir Galahad and Huxley's death. She wouldn't be here otherwise."

"Did she follow us?" Becky wondered aloud. "Or was she coming down here anyway, and we just happened to run across her?"

Neither of them had an answer for that. Flynn finally nudged the parcel that the woman had dropped down with the toe of his boot. "Shall we see what she left us?"

"We might as well. You never know, there might be something that can help us get out of here."

But the bundle, when unwrapped, proved to be the slightly squashed remains of a picnic lunch: packets of sandwiches wrapped in paper, iced biscuits, three lemon tarts, and a metal thermos full of what smelled like tea.

They spread everything out on the ground, and then the squirrel—which had been quietly nursing its grievances up until now—suddenly darted forward, seized one of the biscuits, and retreated back to the corner to devour its prize.

"Well, I suppose that will at least say whether she was telling the truth about the food being all right," Flynn said, eyeing the shower of crumbs that was dropping from the small animal's jaws.

That seemed slightly callous, but on the other hand, Becky couldn't think of a way of getting the biscuit—what was left of it—away from the squirrel without getting clawed or bitten for her trouble.

"What did you think about her?" Becky asked. She had her own opinions about the woman, and usually she wasn't afraid to trust her gut instincts. But in this case, she was uncertain enough to honestly want to hear what Flynn had to say before she even tried to make up her mind.

"She talks a bit like Lucy."

"You're right. She's American. At least, if that accent was her real one. She sounded English when she came to the door to talk to me."

Her accent had been very well done, too. Maybe Lucy or Mr. Holmes could have spotted that it was faked, but Becky hadn't been able to tell.

"But I mean, what do you think about what she said?" Becky asked.

Flynn's brows edged together. "I don't know," he said slowly. "She's right. We don't have any reason to believe a word that came out of her mouth. And yet, you know, I got the feeling she was telling the truth. A lot of the time, anyway. For one thing, I don't think she's the one who attacked us and put us down here."

"I thought that, too," Becky said. "I would swear that she wasn't acting. She really was surprised to see us when she opened the trap door. So how do we feel about her promising to send help back for us?"

Flynn tilted his head. "Seems like a pointless lie, if it was a lie. I mean, what were we going to do to her, even if she didn't promise to send a rescue? We're stuck down here. Nothing for her to fear from us, no way we could have stopped her from just walking away without promising anything at all."

That was depressingly true—especially the part about their being trapped.

Becky forced that thought out of her mind. The way to tackle any problem, no matter how overwhelming, was one step at a time. That was what Lucy always said. "All right," she said. "What about the food? Do you think it's safe for us to eat?"

She wasn't hungry now, but there was no telling how long they might be down here.

Flynn frowned again, then shrugged. "Nothing ventured." He picked up one of the sandwiches and started to unwrap it.

"Flynn!"

Flynn started, almost dropping the sandwich. "What? Doesn't seem to have done him any harm, anyway." He jabbed a thumb in the direction of the squirrel, which was still gnawing on biscuit crumbs in the corner.

"No—I mean, yes, but that wasn't what I meant. Look at the wrapping paper."

Flynn picked up the outer layer of paper that the sandwich had been wrapped in and held it up. On the outer side it was plain white, but the other side—the one that had caught Becky's attention—was covered with writing.

He squinted at it. "Looks like … a letter? Or the start of one."

He handed the sheet over to Becky, who read aloud:

"*My dear sister,*

I am in considerable distress of mind at the rumours that have reached me about Mr. Huxley. I should hate to attach importance to what may be only ill-natured gossip, and of course as an employer, Mr. Huxley has never been anything but respectful and polite to me, with nothing improper in—"

Becky stopped.

"Nothing improper in what?" Flynn asked.

"I don't know. That's where the letter stops. Look." She held up the page so that he could see the unfinished final line. "Maybe whoever was writing the letter got interrupted? Or—look." She pointed to a slight brown discoloration across the bottom of the page. "That looks as though it could be a tea stain. The woman writing it could have spilled tea on it accidentally, then thrown this page away and started over again."

"Woman?"

"The handwriting is definitely a woman's," Becky said. She frowned. "And it sounds like whoever she is, she worked for Mr. Huxley. She calls him her employer."

"So who is she? Our friend with the red hair?"

"I doubt it." Becky shook her head decidedly. "I don't see her working at a bank, do you?"

"Maybe not. How'd she get hold of this paper, then?" Flynn asked.

"I don't know. The real question is, Why would she toss it down here to us?"

"Accident?" Flynn suggested. "She may not have realized she'd done it."

"She just happened to have a partial letter about Mr. Huxley, our murder victim, and thought, *Oh, well, I might as well wrap my sandwiches for today's picnic in it*?" Becky gave him a withering look. "Besides, she doesn't seem to me like the kind of person who does anything by accident."

"All right. So she wanted us to have the letter for some reason," Flynn said. "Why? A rumour about Mr. Huxley? What's that supposed to mean?"

"I don't know. We need to tell Mr. Holmes about this." Becky's hands curled in frustration as she eyed the distance between them and the trapdoor overhead—which unluckily for them hadn't gotten any smaller in the last half hour. "But for that, we need to find a way out of here."

CHAPTER 18: LUCY

The usual clicks and whirs and crackles as I waited for the telephone exchange to put me through to Baker Street seemed to take an age, and I had to stop myself from tapping my fingers on the edge of Dr. Norton's desk. Jack would see the motion and know that I was uneasy—and I wanted to keep from infecting him with my sense of crawling, nameless worry.

I wasn't even sure where the anxiety was stemming from. True, Jack had been injured. But he'd had worse hurts than a gash in the arm, and we'd both been in far more dangerous situations than this one appeared, at least on the surface.

At last, my call went through, and Holmes's voice came on the line.

"Ah, Lucy. I am thankful that you called."

Instantly, my uneasiness increased tenfold, blossoming into full-blown worry. Holmes never spoke of his emotional state out loud. To have him admit to a feeling of thankfulness meant that something was seriously wrong.

"What's happened?" I asked at once.

Jack had been helping Dr. Norton to clean up the remaining scattered papers, but looked up sharply at my tone.

Holmes's voice was calmly measured when he answered, but I caught the undercurrent of tension in his words all the same.

"As yet, I am not aware of anything untoward that has

occurred. But Flynn and Becky failed to turn up at Baker Street this afternoon as I had asked, which, after I had telephoned and received no answer, prompted me to send Charlie, one of the other irregulars, to investigate. Your house is empty, save for the dog Prince. Flynn and Becky are nowhere to be found."

* * *

"At least we can be pretty sure that Becky and Flynn are together," Jack said.

We had departed from Dr. Norton's and were walking quickly through the town towards the train station. The streets were emptier now, with the day's business winding down, and most people already at home for their supper hour.

"That's supposed to make me feel better? You know what the two of them are like in combination! They've gotten themselves into every kind of trouble imaginable by now."

"To be fair, they usually manage to get themselves out of it again," Jack said.

His calm wasn't because he didn't care about his younger sister. But he'd raised Becky on his own from the time her mother died when she was seven, and knew even better than I did the futility of trying to keep her out of danger.

I had to admit that he was right. Becky and Flynn might get themselves into one hair-raising scrape after another, but somehow managed to walk away relatively unharmed. That didn't mean that their luck wouldn't run out eventually, but it did allow me to think more clearly.

"Where do you think they'll have gone?" I asked Jack.

Jack's brows drew together. "At a guess? They'll have decided to tackle some angle of this case—Mr. Huxley's murder—on their own."

"That would mean that they came here, to Tottenham."

"I'd say it's the most likely spot to start looking, at any rate." Jack hesitated, glancing at me, then said, "I'd also bet that they were planning to be back in time to meet you and your father at Baker Street."

He was right about that, too. Becky and Flynn could have posed for a portrait illustration of the old saw about it being easier to beg forgiveness than ask permission. But they would have wanted to avoid getting scolded for going off alone and without telling anyone where they were going, if at all possible.

"So the fact that they're not at 221B now—"

"Means that something went wrong," Jack finished for me. Grimness tightened the line of his mouth, although his voice was still calm.

I forced down the grip of anxiety and nodded towards the train station just ahead of us. "Well, at least there's an easy way to start looking for confirmation that they really did come here. We can ask whether any of the attendants at the station noticed them arrive on one of the afternoon trains."

That proved easier said than done, however. Jack and I split up so that we could cover more ground, and I spoke to three porters, two who were harried and busy with shuttling luggage on and off the trains, and one who was frankly lazy and trying to shirk as much work as possible by lounging in the shelter of one of the platform benches.

None of them recalled seeing a pair of children answering Flynn's and Becky's description. I was raising my voice while questioning the third porter, trying to be heard above the noise of the train that had just come chugging in to the station, when a woman passing by stopped in mid-step and turned to me.

"Did you say you're looking for a boy and a girl?"

She was dressed all in white, with a wide-brimmed straw hat set atop red hair. Her accent held a faint trace of the American south, and I noted automatically that her white kid shoes bore traces of mud and dried leaves, and that she had at some point during the day been eating strawberry ice cream.

Although I cared less in the moment about those details than about what she'd just said.

"Yes, have you seen them?"

She bit her lip. "I think so. We were ... that is, I believe I saw a blond-haired boy and girl arrive on the same train that I did. The last I saw them, they were walking up towards the castle—I assumed they were planning to visit the fair there."

"Thank you."

The woman nodded, glanced at me quickly, then hurried to scramble up into one of the waiting train cars.

"Did you hear that?" I turned to Jack, who had come up to stand beside me.

He nodded. "At least we know now that we're on the right track."

"I'd forgotten about the fair. But Becky knew about it. She showed me a newspaper clipping. She was especially excited about the carousel."

"And they'd both know that they'd stand a better chance of blending in and going unnoticed in a crowd of other kids all playing the fair games and riding the carousel."

"Which means our next port of call should be the castle."

"That won't do us much good unless we have a plan first for how we're going to approach them up there."

As much as I wanted to hire the first available cab and drive straight to Galahad's Castle in hopes of finding Flynn and Becky, I had to admit that Jack was right.

"Especially after everything that Dr. Norton just told us about Sir Galahad and his first wife. Do you think he did murder her?"

"Just going on what Dr. Norton said, I don't for the moment see how he'd have managed it," Jack said. "But if you're asking whether her falling off the castle tower was an accident, I'd say not. Whether her husband pushed her or convinced her to jump—or whether it was someone else other than him—I'd wager any odds that she didn't die without someone's help."

That was Jack's policeman's intuition talking—the indefinable instinct that those in the law enforcement profession developed, and it was rarely wrong.

"Do you think it was Sir Galahad who broke into Dr. Norton's office today?"

Jack took longer to answer this time, long enough for the train to chug its way out of the station before he said, "We're assuming that Dr. Norton's intruder broke in so that he could steal Rose Trent's case file. But from what Dr. Norton told us, it doesn't sound like there can have been anything to incriminate Sir Galahad in that file. Not any more than the account Dr. Norton himself was able to give us, that is. So why bother breaking in? Why take the risk of getting caught and facing criminal charges, not just for burglary, but for assaulting the doctor?"

That was a good point. I frowned. "Unless there was some detail in the files that Dr. Norton had forgotten about. It has been several years, after all. But you're right. Come to that, why take the further risk of staging the break in during broad daylight, at a time when the office was bound to be occupied? He could just as easily have waited until night, when the place would be empty and he could be almost guaranteed not to run into a soul."

"It almost looks as though he—whoever the intruder was—knew we were coming, and was desperate to take Lady Trent's records before we arrived."

I didn't like that thought at all. "How would he have known that we were coming? Your orders came from Scotland Yard. I told Mr. Huxley's housekeeper where I was going—that is, I asked her for the name of Sir Galahad's doctor. I suppose it's marginally possible that she could have informed Sir Galahad. Whether innocently or because she's in on whatever criminal activity he's currently planning."

"Did you think she was involved when you interviewed her?" Jack asked.

"Not while I was speaking to her. Not now, either, not really. She seems the picture of a typical, middle-aged, more than slightly fussy domestic servant. And genuinely if quietly fond of Mr. Huxley."

Unless she was too typical and both her eccentricities and her affection for her employer had been simply good acting?

I rubbed my forehead. One of the pitfalls of our profession was that one could wind up by seeing hidden motives and sinister forces at work everywhere. "This is an incredibly frustrating murderer we're pursuing."

Jack's smile was brief. "I'm sure he'll apologize when we catch him."

"So how do we want to go about seeing Sir Galahad? If we arrive without warning and knock on the door, we can see whether he has any reaction to seeing you. If he was the intruder you chased away from Dr. Norton's, he ought to recognize you."

Jack looked down at the square of bandage that covered the gash on his arm. But he shook his head. "If we're worried that Flynn and Becky are being held somewhere up at the castle, I think I'm better off staying in the background while you keep them distracted. Or helping with the distraction, so that I can have a look around."

I looked at him sharply. "That sounds as if you already have some kind of a plan for creating a diversion."

Jack nodded slowly. "I do. Although I'll need to use the station's telephone to put through a call. To Nibbs."

"To *Nibbs*?" The man in question was an affable, loose-limbed scarecrow of an East-End Londoner who had—after a spectacularly unsuccessful career as a petty criminal—turned to work as a police informant. He also had all the moral fiber of a scavenging hyena—if that much.

"I'm not sure which should worry me more," I said. "The fact that Becky and Flynn are missing, or the fact that your plan for finding them apparently starts with the words, *Put through a call to Nibbs.*"

Jack smiled again. It was a hard-edged smile, but he put his arm around me. "Think you're the only one who can come up with crazy ideas?"

Chapter 19: Flynn

Flynn groped his way along the back wall of the cellar. This far away from the narrow shaft of light from the trapdoor, it was almost pitch black, and he shuffled his feet and kept his hands straight out in front of him to avoid tripping or running into the wall.

"Find anything?" Becky called from the other side.

"Yeah, there's a back door over here. I just didn't think to mention it," Flynn muttered. He'd been trapped in unpleasant underground places before this, and he'd reached the now familiar stage where he started to picture the weight of all the tons of earth on top of them. His lungs felt tight, and his skin was hot and prickling despite the cold, dank air.

Becky ignored him and said, "There's nothing at all over here. Although the walls feel like they're made of dirt. If we had enough time, we might be able to dig our way out."

"Using what? Our bare hands? An army of trained moles?"

He couldn't see Becky's face, since she was just a vague shadow in the dark. But he heard her blow out an annoyed-sounding breath. "Fine, what have you found?"

"I told you, nothing—" Flynn started, then broke off as his outstretched hands suddenly connected with something "Hold on."

"What is it?"

"Not sure." Flynn felt around in the darkness again, running his hands across a rough wooden surface. "I think it's some kind of a shelf, mounted on the wall back here. Wait." He stooped and felt down lower. "Yeah, there's a couple of them. The wall is brick, not wood, and there's a pair of wooden shelves attached."

"That would make sense."

Flynn almost jumped at Becky's voice coming from so close this time, and realized she'd crossed the cellar to stand beside him.

"My guess is that we're in the root cellar of that little cottage place we found."

"Why?"

"Because whoever locked us in here couldn't have carried us very far—not without risking someone seeing them. So if we're in a root cellar, it was probably once used for storing crops—carrots and potatoes and all that kind of thing. Is there anything on the shelves?"

Becky stepped nearer, reaching to feel them for herself.

"Not that I've found." Flynn ran a hand across the top shelf, then jerked back. "Ouch! No, nothing but splinters that I can find."

Becky sighed. "That's that, then. I kept thinking that there had to be something down here that would help us get out. Because of what the red-haired woman said about betting that we'd be free by the time she sent help back. I thought she must have seen something from up there that we hadn't found yet. But maybe I'm giving her too much credit—"

"What about the shelves?" Flynn interrupted.

"What?"

"The shelves. They're sturdy and made of wood. And a good six feet long, at least."

"If you're thinking of building a ladder—" Becky began.

"Not a ladder. But I'll bet if we could get one down from

here, we could prop it up against the wall near the trapdoor like a ramp. Then we can climb up."

Becky was silent, and Flynn sensed her staring at him.

"What? You think you're the only one who can come up with crazy plans?" he asked.

"That's not even so crazy," Becky said. "It might actually work."

"Only if we really can get one of the shelves off of here. Come on."

Working together, they took hold of the upper wooden shelf and started tugging. It had been bolted in place, but so long ago that the screws were practically rusted through, and Flynn felt them start to give almost right away.

"Pull!"

They yanked and pulled, and finally staggered back as the shelf came free in a shower of crumbling mortar.

"All right." Becky wiped dust out of her eyes. "Let's see how close this can get us to the trapdoor."

It took a bit of engineering, but finally by digging a shallow trench in the floor to brace the bottom end of the shelf, they were able to lean the slab of wood up against the wall so that the end rested only about three feet away from the edge of the trapdoor.

"I'd better go first," Becky said, eyeing the arrangement. "You're heavier than I am. We don't want to risk the board cracking on the first try."

"You sure?" Flynn asked.

He knew better than to suggest that Becky should think again or let him go first. But while he was used to jumping across roof tops and scrambling up outside walls to second-story windows on jobs for Mr. Holmes, he had a feeling that heights weren't Becky's favorite thing. Even if she'd never admit it.

"Of course I'm sure." She swallowed. "I'll be fine. Just hold the board steady for me."

Flynn did as she said, crouching down and planting his knees and hands on the end of the board to keep it from rocking or tipping sideways.

Becky took a breath and started to scramble up the ramp, pulling herself hand over hand. The board creaked in protest, but it didn't break, and finally she reached the top where the upper end rested against the wall.

"All right. Now I just have to see if I can reach the door."

She swiveled in place carefully, stretching out an arm.

Flynn thought of something. "How are you going to unfasten the latch from the inside?"

He'd heard the red-haired woman shoot it into place before she left.

"It's all right, I've got my pocket knife," Becky said. "Lucy gave it to me and said to always carry it in case of emergency." Still balancing carefully, she reached into her coat pocket, brought out the knife, and flicked open the blade. "I think I ought to be able to force the latch up."

She leaned towards the trapdoor, carefully wriggling the blade into the space between the wood panel and the frame. She wobbled for a second, and the board tried to tilt under her weight. Flynn threw all his weight into holding it down, but it still wanted to tip sideways, all the while creaking ominously.

"Hurry up, I'm not sure how long this wood will hold."

"Oh, good idea, I would never have thought of that," Becky growled back.

She fiddled another minute or two that seemed to take a lot longer than the usual sixty seconds. But then, finally, Flynn heard a click of metal, and Becky called out, "I've got it!"

"That's good, can you push the door up?"

"I'm … trying."

Becky had to lean out even farther to get enough leverage to push the trapdoor out of the way, and Flynn was certain she was going to end up pitching off the ramp and onto the floor.

"There," she said at last. "That's done it."

Looking up, Flynn saw that the flap was lifted, leaving an open square of blue sky visible above them.

"Good work. I'll hold the board steady while you climb out. Then I'll come up."

Becky nodded, but turned to look back at him over her shoulder. "Are you sure you can manage with no one to hold the ramp steady for you?"

"I'll have to, won't I? At the least, once you're out, you can go find help—or a rope, whichever's closer."

"All right." Taking a breath, Becky straightened and stood up, balancing precariously on the wooden beam. She wobbled a bit again, but managed to catch hold of the trapdoor's frame, and with some scrambling, pull herself up and out.

"Your turn." Turning, she crouched to put her face into the hole and look down at him.

"Right."

Flynn made it up the ramp all right. He'd had to walk along enough narrow ledges and windowsills that balancing on a wooden shelf wasn't any great challenge. But when he was almost to the top, he felt the board crack under him.

He'd have fallen, but instinct made him jump the remaining distance and grab hold of the edges of the trap door frame. Although once he was there, he realized maybe his instincts needed a couple of pointers on common sense. Because he was dangling with his legs in the air, and not enough of a grip to haul himself up and out of the cellar. It was all he could do just to hang on.

"Here, grab hold." Lying flat on the ground outside, Becky stretched out her hands to him.

He wasn't sure she'd be strong enough to pull him, but he shifted his hands one at a time to grip hers.

Becky gritted her teeth as she started to wriggle her way backwards, pulling him with her.

"Hang on."

"Oh, good idea, never would have thought of that."

She rolled her eyes, but kept pulling, and finally he was up far enough that he could brace his feet on the edge of the trap door frame and scramble up the rest of the way.

A few seconds later, they were both lying flat on their backs on the dusty ground next to the trapdoor, staring up at the sky and trying to catch their breaths.

Something squeaked nearby, which made Flynn sit up. The squirrel ran up the ramp, leapt for the edge of the trapdoor, clung a moment, then executed a complicated twist that sent it up over the edge and onto solid ground. Still chattering in an annoyed-sounding way, it scampered off into the surrounding forest, disappearing into the trees.

"That's gratitude for you," Flynn said.

Becky shrugged. "I'd have felt guilty if it had been trapped down in the cellar. It was my fault it was down there in the first place."

"So what now?" Flynn asked. "Back to the train station so that we can tell Mr. Holmes about all of this? We can probably still catch the last train of the day."

Becky tilted her head to look up at the sun, which was rapidly sinking in a blaze of fiery red along the horizon. But she shook her head.

"I was right. We are near the cottage, look."

She pointed. They were behind a small cluster of maples, but through them, maybe 20 feet away, Flynn could see the cottage they'd been about to search when they'd been attacked. It looked empty and dark in the growing late afternoon shadows, just like before.

"So?" He already had an uncomfortable feeling about where this was leading.

"We do need to report back to Mr. Holmes," Becky said. "But first, I want to see what we can find out about the person who locked us down there."

Chapter 20: Lucy

"Hello, fair lady."

The tall man in the manor house doorway showed his perfect teeth in an engaging smile. "I am Galahad."

I had been curious as to what Sir Galahad would be like in person, and at first glance, he certainly lived up to his reputation for eccentricity. He was clothed entirely in rich fabrics of Lincoln green and in Elizabethan style, as if he had just stepped away from a meeting with the Tudor queen and her most fashionable courtiers. Dark-haired, handsome, probably a few years shy of forty, he radiated confidence and a lifetime of privilege.

He also didn't look even slightly perturbed to see me. Or as though he had been breaking into Dr. Norton's office and slashing my husband with a dagger an hour earlier. But first impressions were notoriously unreliable.

"Answering my own door, as you can see," he went on. "Bit unusual, but there you are. I take it you walked through all the historical hubbub behind you?"

He made a sweeping gesture towards the colorful bustle on his wide, park-like front lawn, where, although evening was fast approaching, a village costume fair was still in full swing. Vendors cried shrilly as they hawked their wares; villagers clustered around the stalls; cooks hunched over ovens and tables piled high with pastries. Here and there minstrels with lutes wandered, singing madrigal tunes, their melodies barely audible amid the din. The painted wooden horses on a steam-powered carousel were the only objects not in motion, and they had just stopped to take on another load of eager children.

"I managed to make my way," I said.

"Splendid. Now, I take it you are Miss James, sent here by the bank. What can I do for you?"

"Why the green costume?" I heard myself asking.

He positively beamed. "A remarkably astute question. I represent a character renowned in Arthurian lore known as the Green Knight."

I had read the ancient poem in school. "The famous knight who was able to survive decapitation with an ax and ride away with his head tucked under one arm?"

Galahad doffed his green cap and made a courtly bow. "I salute your erudition, Miss James. Yes, indeed, I emulate the fabled Green Knight. The giant who taught the court of King Arthur a painful lesson concerning the essence of knightly chivalry. And do you know what that essence is, Miss James?" He went on without giving me the chance to reply. "Resilience—enough to survive getting one's head struck off. Personal honor—keeping one's word, even when it means sacrificing one's own life. And above all, showing the highest respect for womanhood."

"An admirable code to live by."

As I spoke, I studied Sir Galahad's figure again, deciding that he wasn't just eccentric. I'd spent a good deal of my first years in London immersed in the world of the theater, and right now the impression I had of the Earl of Trent was that of a man on the stage, playing a theatrical part, and enjoying his own performance thoroughly.

What lay beneath the play-acting, though—that I wasn't yet sure of.

"Thank you," he said. "At any rate, those are the virtues that I strive to exemplify, and to teach to our British countrymen in this somewhat indelicate age. And"—he stepped back, pushing the door open wide with a flourish—"these are my knights."

Eight tough-faced, muscular men stood around a large wooden table, shadowy figures behind high-backed wooden chairs. Eight impassive faces and eight pairs of eyes stared at me with a stolid, fixed regard that made the muscles in my neck and shoulders tense.

I wasn't usually intimidated by an opponent's strength or size in a potential fight. But even still, a crawling awareness went through me of how isolated and alone I was at the moment—and how ugly this could get if Sir Galahad commanded his knights to attack.

According to Mrs. Lambe, their usual targets were men who mistreated their wives. But none of the men before me looked as though they were strangers to other types of violence.

Galahad cleared his throat. "This concerns my construction loan, I take it?" He gestured at the barren interior. "Has my application been approved?"

"May I come in?" I asked.

"Of course. Let us have a cup of tea in our great hall."

The eight men dispersed. Galahad motioned me to a chair.

Despite its imposing title, the great hall itself was barren, cavernous, as if it were a great barn for farm animals. The walls were bare wooden lath; the floors were dusty, unfinished wooden planks. There was no ceiling where the 'knights' now stood. Looking upwards, I could see daylight coming through small dusty windows that had, I realized, once been accessible only from the upper floor. One of the men returned with a tea cart and poured—which would have been comical, if I'd been in the mood to find anything humorous. At the moment, though, even the sight of a hulking six-foot man in knight's costume playing the part of a parlor maid couldn't distract me from the fact that Flynn and Becky were missing. Or from the need to approach this meeting with care.

I balanced my cup and saucer, weighing my options. Usually I dreaded having to break the news of a murder to the victim's friends or loved ones. But neither Mr. Huxley nor Mrs. Clair had been particular friends of Sir Galahad. And there were times when the shock value of a direct approach could startle a witness into more honest answers than they might otherwise have given.

"I'm afraid I must tell you that the two people processing your loan application at the bank have been murdered," I said.

Then again, shock value only worked if the witness you were interrogating was capable of being shocked.

Sir Galahad frowned. "But will that interfere with the funding?"

"That depends on another matter."

"Which is?"

"Your father-in-law believes you're about to murder your wife."

I had expected an outburst of some sort: rage, offended dignity, vigorous denial and a pledge of undying love for his current wife. What I saw was a casual shrug and a twitch of irritation in the line of his mouth.

"Ah. I take it my beloved father-in-law is still on about Rose, is he? My first wife? As if it weren't tragedy enough, he's been acting as though it's a guilty secret. The subject comes up every time Carlotta—my wife, that is—asks him for more money. Which she does, of course. Got so bad I asked the bank for a loan to finish this project. Just so I wouldn't have to listen to more of his sanctimonious insinuations."

"I understand Lady Trent went to the bank with him two days ago."

"Yes, Carlotta told me. Splendid fellow, Huxley." Sir Galahad appeared to belatedly realize that his reaction to the news of Huxley's murder had been somewhat lacking, because he added, with an awkward grimace, "Sorry he's dead. Sorry about Mrs. Clair, too."

"Why did Carlotta go to the bank with her father?"

"Probably wanted to keep the old fool from mucking up our loan." Galahad looked thoughtful for a moment. "But surely it would be far easier for you to ask Carlotta herself."

He rapped his spoon against the teapot. One of the knights appeared in the doorway from which the tea cart had emerged, which I took to be the kitchen. "Sir?"

"Is Lady Trent at home?"

Chapter 21: Lucy

Before meeting her, I had unconsciously formed a mental picture of Lady Carlotta Trent as being of a similar type as the first Lady Trent: a spoiled, wealthy heiress who had married Sir Galahad for the sake of the title, and was now trapped—bored, probably discontented, but unable to do anything but grudgingly acquiesce to her husband's eccentricities.

The real Lady Trent exploded that imaginary person from the moment she came into the room.

"Yes, darling?" she asked her husband. Her accent was American, but her voice was nearly toneless and so quiet that I had to strain to hear. "You wanted to see me?"

Carlotta Trent wasn't beautiful, but then, neither was she plain. She was a small, colorless woman who looked to be somewhere in her late twenties, with mouse-brown hair that hung in loose waves held in place by a golden coronet that circled her forehead. The style was undoubtedly meant to convey an Arthurian atmosphere, but it also entirely overwhelmed her small, pale face, just as the gown of rich crimson velvet and gold brocade she wore seemed to entirely engulf her narrow frame.

Keeping one's mind free from any preconceived prejudice was essential in any investigation, and despite her father's worries, I had been mentally giving Sir Galahad the benefit of the doubt. But unfortunately for him, Carlotta Trent looked to be exactly the kind of girl whom men would marry for the sake of her money.

"Miss James has some questions about your father, my dear," Sir Galahad said.

"About Daddy?" Carlotta looked startled and cast a quick, nervous glance at me. "There's nothing wrong, is there? Nothing's happened to him?"

With Sir Galahad, I had been willing to employ shock tactics, and goodness knew that by this point in my career as an investigator, I was used to uncomfortable and even violent conversations.

But even still, it was hard to imagine telling Carlotta, *Your father suspects your husband of planning to murder you.*

"No, nothing like that," I said. "I'm here in connection with the death of Mr. Huxley, whom I believe you and your father went to see at Tottenham Bank recently?"

"Oh." Carlotta looked still more startled, then swallowed. "That is, yes. Yes, we did."

Evidently she was going to be one of those witnesses who dispensed with information as readily as a miser did his pennies.

"May I ask what your father said to Huxley about Sherlock Holmes?" I asked.

This time, Carlotta's nervous glance was directed at her husband before she answered. "He … He wanted Mr. Huxley to send Mr. Holmes ten thousand dollars. Daddy was taking the boat back to Cleveland so he wouldn't be around to write a check." A frown crossed her brow. "Wait a moment. Did you say that Mr. Huxley was *dead*?"

"I'm afraid so. He was killed last night."

"Killed?" Carlotta's face blanched. "How dreadful! I can't

think who'd have wanted to harm him. I only met him once, but he seemed such a nice man."

"Do you know why your father wished Mr. Huxley to set up the retainer for Mr. Holmes?" I asked.

I was watching Carlotta carefully, wondering exactly how much of his suspicions her father had shared. But her gaze remained wide-eyed and entirely clear.

"Oh, yes. That is, only generally. Daddy wanted Sherlock Holmes to look into some business associates of his here in England—a shipping firm that he was thinking of going into business with. But he wanted to make sure that they were trustworthy before signing any contracts."

"I see." That answered the question of how much of his suspicions her father had shared. "Did you father and Mr. Huxley discuss anything else?"

"Well—" Carlotta stopped, fiddling nervously with a golden tassel that decorated the overskirt of her gown.

"It's all right, my dear." Galahad said. "You can speak freely. I won't be annoyed."

Despite the reassurance—or because of it?—Carlotta looked still more nervous, nor did she meet her husband's gaze as she said, all in a rush, "They talked about Galahad's Castle and the construction loan from the bank. That's why Galahad made me ... that is, that's why I went with Daddy to the meeting. Mr. Huxley was trying to get Daddy to support the project, and we hoped if I was there to back him up, Daddy might agree to guarantee the loan, or at least some of the loan."

"And did he agree?"

"Well, no. No, I'm afraid he didn't. But Mr. Huxley was willing to give Galahad the loan anyway, even if Daddy didn't guarantee it," Carlotta added hurriedly. "So it really wasn't such a blow as it might have been."

Watching how Sir Galahad's face darkened at even her account of the meeting, I doubted that.

Carlotta cast a quick look at the door, as though looking for an escape route.

"Is that all you wanted to know, Miss James?"

I smiled sympathetically. "I know all of these questions are tedious to answer. But I'm afraid the police will ask them anyway, whenever they come to interview you about Mr. Huxley's death. You were among the last people to see Huxley alive, so far as we've been able to find out. Did he seem upset or worried?"

"No. At least …"

Her voice trailed off.

"At least?" I finally prompted.

"Nothing." Carlotta swallowed again. "Nothing at all. He seemed perfectly normal the whole time we were talking to him."

Whatever other talents Carlotta Trent might possess, the ability to lie convincingly wasn't one of them. But I didn't think there was anything to be gained by pressing her. At least, not in front of her husband.

"And what happened after the interview?"

"Nothing, really. Huxley escorted Daddy and me out of the bank and saw us safely on board a cab. Then we came back here for supper. In the east wing, of course, not here."

"Our renovation will transform it," Galahad said.

"Of course." Carlotta gave her husband another quick, frightened glance. "I'm sorry, dearest, I didn't mean that … I mean, I didn't mean anything! A few months from now, it will be glorious. But Daddy and I ate in the dining room as usual. You remember? We were at table when you and the rest of the staff came back from setting up the fair."

"And when did you begin setting up the fair that afternoon?" I asked.

Sir Galahad looked puzzled. "Why?"

"Just a routine question." Also, I needed to prolong this conversation long enough for Jack to begin his distraction. We were fortunate in that the train service between London and Tottenham was only a matter of twenty minutes or so. But we still needed to wait for everything to be in place and ready for him.

I kept my pleasant smile firmly in place, and added, "The police will want to check on everyone's whereabouts, so that they can eliminate anyone who has an alibi for Mr. Huxley's death."

"We started just after lunch. I'm sure my staff will be able to vouch for me," Galahad said.

He spoke with complete confidence, which could mean that his alibi was true. Or it could equally mean that he knew the odds of one of his servants risking their livelihood by contradicting him were exactly nil.

Mrs. Lambe had spoken of Sir Galahad's personal crusade to champion the downtrodden women of Tottenham. Dr. Norton, who had known him since boyhood, had conveyed the impression that Sir Galahad might be idealistic and selectively blind—even naïve. But nothing he'd said had suggested that Lord Trent was either cruel or a tyrant.

Yet here and now, Galahad's own wife definitely seemed to be, if not outright afraid of him, at least extremely nervous in his presence.

"Oh, and then there was the reporter," Sir Galahad added.

"Reporter?"

"Yes. A woman. She came while we were setting up to interview me. Said she was going to do a big write-up piece about the fair in her paper's society pages."

The back of my neck prickled. "Did she say which newspaper she was from?"

"Did she now?" Sir Galahad frowned. "I suppose she must have done, but I can't remember. The Times? No, it wasn't that one. But I showed her around the fairgrounds a bit, told her about what we were trying to do. Oh, and I showed her my collection, as well."

"Collection?"

"Yes, the artifacts we've unearthed from the archaeological digs on the grounds. Got some fine specimens of medieval weapons—arrowheads, an ax or two. Even a sword. She seemed very interested—wrote down everything I said, and promised to come back with a photographer when the fair was open."

"And did she?" I asked.

"I'm not sure. Merlin might know. He was helping me with running everything. He'll be here in a bit to take dinner with us, as usual, if you want to ask him about her. Why? Do you think it matters?"

"It could." I had no proof, of course, that anything about the reporter's visit was significant. But in my head, an echo of Mrs. Lambe the housekeeper's voice was playing, highlighting words I hadn't paid nearly enough attention to at the time.

You wouldn't believe the trouble I've had with the newspaper reporters! Why, I found one of them rooting through the trash! Simply shameless, she was.

Female reporters were less uncommon than they'd been twenty or even ten years ago, and it was entirely possible that one might have been assigned to cover the fair at Galahad's castle. Newspaper editors rarely assigned the women on their staff to murder investigations, though.

The reporter who'd outraged Mrs. Lambe and the one who'd interviewed Sir Galahad could be two different women. But somehow I doubted it.

A ring of the front doorbell broke the moment's silence. I heard voices out in the front hallway, and then one of Sir Galahad's knights appeared in the doorway.

"There's a bloke here with the police," he grunted. I'd yet to hear any of the knights speak, and this one sounded a good deal more as though he hailed from Whitechapel in the East End of London than Camelot.

He stepped aside to reveal Jack, propelling a man in handcuffs into the room.

"Lord Trent?" Jack asked. At Sir Galahad's nod, he said, "My name is Sergeant Kelly, from Scotland Yard. I was coming here with a few questions regarding Mr. Huxley the banker's death when I caught this man trying to break into one of your ground-floor windows."

Chapter 22: Becky

For once, Flynn wasn't arguing with her about the plan. Instead, it was the small, sensible voice in the back of Becky's head that was fighting with her, pointing out that if Lucy had gotten back home—or if Jack was home from Scotland Yard—they would be worried when they found she was gone. Moreover, it was stupid to stay here when the person who'd locked them in the root cellar could be back any time.

But on the other hand, if Lucy and Jack were home, then they were already worried. At least Becky could make sure that this trip didn't turn out to be a waste of time. Because they'd tracked someone from Mr. Huxley's house to this cottage, and whoever it was had knocked them both unconscious to stop them from finding out any more about the place.

Becky wanted to know why. And if they left and came back later with Lucy or Jack or Mr. Holmes, they might be safer, but there was also no telling what kind of evidence the person they'd tracked here would have had time to destroy.

Flynn must have seen that too, because he'd agreed to her proposal that they search the cottage. His only condition had been that they stick together this time.

So they were creeping carefully through the trees, up towards the cottage's painted front door.

Flynn was sniffing the air. "Do you smell burning again?"

Becky inhaled and nodded. The smokey smell was stronger than before, and although she couldn't identify where it was coming from, she could smell something else besides the smoke.

"It smells like whoever started the fire used kerosene to start it."

"So what do we do?" Flynn asked. "Try to find out who was burning what, or have a look around the cottage?"

Becky debated. "Cottage first."

"What do we do if someone's home?"

"Run?" That was the best idea she had.

"Fine."

They reached the square of red sandstone that served as the cottage's front step. Becky stretched out a hand, about to try the door—then realized that it was actually already open a crack.

She gave it a push and it swung wide, with a creak that sounded loud enough not just to alert anyone inside, but to summon anyone else who happened to be within a mile radius, as well. Nothing happened, though.

The room inside the cottage—as much of it as she could see, anyway—was dim, quiet, and empty. Birds were chirping in the trees all around, but otherwise the woods were silent.

Becky glanced questioningly back at Flynn, who shrugged. "In for a penny, in for a pound?"

As sayings went, that one had never seemed particularly sensible to her. But she nodded and stepped across the threshold.

The air inside the cottage smelled strange: an herbal, earthy scent that Becky couldn't identify. It set her teeth on edge, somehow, and judging by Flynn's tense shoulders, he felt the same. But at least no one jumped out at them from the shadows.

The shutters were all closed up tight, and with the sun setting outside, not much light came in through the doorway behind them, either. It was a moment or two before Becky's eyes could adjust to the dimness and begin to make out details of the room. There was almost no furniture, just a lot of baskets and burlap sacks piled in heaps on the floor. A long table stretched across the whole back wall, and it was covered with pots and glass jars and a strange apparatus made of pipes and rubber tubes and a gas burner.

"Looks like Mr. Holmes's chemistry setup," Flynn murmured.

It did. Which made Becky more uneasy still. What was a lot of complicated laboratory equipment doing out here, in an abandoned cottage in the middle of the woods?

"Sir Galahad said that they had an archaeology dig going on here. Maybe this is all something to do with that?" she suggested. She'd read an article once about how archaeologists used acids and chemicals and things to strip the dirt away from their finds.

"Think Sir Galahad's the one who tossed us down in the cellar?" Flynn asked.

"I don't know." Becky tried to picture the hooded figure they'd been following. But it was difficult; the cape he'd worn made it hard for her guess at exact details like height and build. "There's no point in trying to decide that now," she said. "We need to see whether there's anything to find here and then get out, before Sir Galahad or anyone else comes back."

Flynn shifted his weight uneasily. "Speaking of that, are we sure we don't want to just head straight for the train station? Nothing good ever comes from messing around in a place like this."

"We're not looking for *good*, we're looking for information."

Flynn blew out a breath, but started in hunting through the assortment of piles ranged around and underneath the long worktable.

"So what exactly are we looking for?"

Becky couldn't answer that. "We'll know it if we find it?"

"Oh, wonderful." Flynn kept working, though, peering into baskets and shaking out sacks. "Looks like just a lot of plants to me."

A bulb that looked a bit like an onion fell out of the sack he was holding and bounced on the floor.

Becky was finding more of the same. She'd started looking around and examining the setup on the worktable, and discovered that most of the jars and pots held what looked like herbs or dried leaves or chopped up mushrooms. All different colored liquids filled the glass vials, ranging from pale green to a murky, inky black.

"What do you think all this is for? Not archaeology, obviously."

Flynn set down another burlap sack and straightened, frowning. "The real question is: why'd someone go to all the trouble of knocking us out and locking us in the cellar to stop us from getting a look in here?"

He was right. The contents of the cottage were odd, certainly. But so far there was nothing illegal or incriminating about them that she could see.

"Wait a second." Something under the work table had caught Becky's eye: a square of white paper that stood out against the dark floorboards. She crouched down and picked it up.

"What is it?" Flynn asked.

"I'm not sure." What she had taken for paper had turned out to be a photograph. Becky crossed to the partially open doorway and held it up to catch the last of the light from the setting sun outside.

The image captured was of two children, a boy and a girl, standing side by side in front of a fireplace. The photograph had clearly been posed. They were both standing with their backs ramrod straight, staring unsmilingly out at the camera.

Flynn came to peer over Becky's shoulder. "Whoever dressed them up like that deserves to be in prison. But apart from that, I don't see what it means."

Becky wasn't surprised Flynn disapproved of their clothes. The boy and girl were dressed up in what had been popular as formal wear in the 1880s. The girl's dress was dripping with lace, with yards and yards of satin pleats in the underskirt, and the bow in her hair was the size of birds' wings. Not a small bird, either. She looked like a giant moth had decided to perch on top of her head. The boy's suit was made of velvet, and was trimmed with almost as much lace as the girl's dress.

"Brother and sister, do you think? But I don't recognize either of them, do you?" she asked Flynn.

Flynn peered at the photograph more closely, but shook his head. "Never seen them before. Although I suppose they'd be grown up by now—"

He broke off at a crash from outside. "What was that?"

"I don't know. It sounded like a branch breaking, maybe?"

They looked at each other, then without speaking, pushed open the door to the cottage and crept outside. It was twilight now, the evening sun gone down and the woods all around them thick with shadows. Bats squeaked and flapped overhead.

"I don't—" *see anything*, Becky was about to whisper.

But before she could finish, Flynn pointed through the trees. "There—look there."

Through the screen of thick branches, Becky caught sight of the orange glow of leaping flames.

"Should we go and have a look?" she whispered.

Flynn was already scowling. "Sure. Why not add one more to the list of bad decisions we've made today?"

But he didn't object when Becky started to pick her way through the trees towards the fire's light. They were both careful not to make any noise, but there was no sign of anyone around. The fire was burning at the center of a ring of pine trees, and there was light enough for Becky to see that the ring was entirely empty. Whoever had started the fire was gone.

"This explains the smoke we were smelling," Flynn murmured.

"And the noise."

The fire had been set in a shallow pit in the ground. A heap of dry branches had been used for kindling, and as they watched, one of them burned through and fell to the ground with a crash and a shower of sparks.

"Why'd someone want to start a fire way out here?" Flynn asked, surveying the blaze.

"To burn something?"

Flynn gave her a look.

"I mean to burn something that they didn't want found, obviously."

Becky took one last look around the circle of pines to make sure they were still alone and then stepped forwards towards the fire. The heat from the flames licked at her face, but she crouched down, trying to see whether she could see anything under the pile of branches.

"It looks like papers, maybe—or what's left of them."

She reached for a scrap, which promptly crumbled away in her fingers to nothing but dust.

"Here's something."

Flynn had taken up a stick from the ground and was digging it into the dirt at the base of the fire pit.

Becky caught sight of a metallic gleam, and then Flynn picked up the object.

"Ow!" He blew on his fingers to cool them, then grabbed for a fold of his shirt to grasp the object without touching it and hold it up so that she could see.

Becky studied the lump of ash-smeared metal. "A key?"

"Looks like it. Should we see if we can find anything else?"

There was nothing especially sinister about the find. But all the same, Becky felt uneasiness prickle all the way up and down her spine. She hadn't been really afraid up until this point, not since they'd gotten out of the cellar. But now the growing darkness seemed to press in like a physical weight from all around, and it suddenly occurred to her that whoever had started the fire might come back.

"No." She shook her head decidedly. "We need to catch the train, get back to London, and show Mr. Holmes everything that we've found."

Chapter 23: Watson

The hour was just after eight o'clock in the evening. I opened the door to our sitting room to admit Preston, the Pinkerton man.

Lestrade already occupied one of our four straight-backed wooden chairs, but Holmes was at the window, looking down on the street below.

He was unlikely to admit it, but I fancied that he was more troubled than he appeared by the fact that Lucy and Jack had not yet returned from Tottenham, and that there was as yet no word as to the whereabouts of Becky and Flynn.

Nevertheless, he turned at Preston's entrance and with a brief wave gestured for him to be seated.

"Thank you for coming, Mr. Preston."

The Pinkerton man acknowledged the greeting with a brief nod. "You have news of the stolen bonds?"

"Perhaps. I hope to know more shortly. But for the moment, I thought it might prove beneficial to pool our findings with regard to the murder of Mr. Huxley."

Preston raised his eyebrows slightly, but said nothing.

Lestrade was the first to speak. "My money would have been on Brown, if it weren't for his alibi."

"Indeed?" Holmes cast another glance out the window.

"Of course. Brown was a suspect, in my opinion, but according to the timetable, he couldn't have killed Mrs. Clair."

"Why suspect Brown?" asked Preston.

"He was the last to see Huxley alive—" Lestrade ticked the points off on his fingers. "And Brown also had a motive. He clearly hated his son-in law. Wanted to thwart the man's ambitions. Blocked the loan by stealing the application papers."

"You believe that derailed the loan?" Holmes asked.

"Well, it has certainly delayed the project. Taken together with Mrs. Clair's murder, especially." Lestrade sighed. "And yet Brown can't be our man, because he was here at Baker Street when Mrs. Clair was murdered in her home in Tottenham."

"Quite true." Holmes's voice was entirely noncommittal, yet I still looked at him sharply. He had some theory that he had not yet voiced, of that I was certain. But I could not guess at what that theory was.

Lestrade appeared to suspect nothing. His narrow shoulders hunched as he added gloomily, "If his alibi were corroborated by anyone else, I'd say it was faked, or that his witness was mistaken. But as it's you, Mr. Holmes ..." he trailed off, looking up at Holmes as though hoping that he might admit to having been mistaken about the time of Brown's visit. When Holmes remained silent, Lestrade heaved another deep sigh. "Right. As it stands, Brown is leaving for America tomorrow, and there's not a thing I can do to stop him."

"His departure is so soon?" Holmes asked.

"Yes." Lestrade looked even more sunk in gloom. "Headed back to Cleveland. Unless"—he looked up at Holmes with a flicker of hope. "Unless you can suggest a way for him to have been here in Baker Street while also murdering Mrs. Clair in Tottenham?"

"I fear not. Although I would ask why, if Brown is guilty, he left those two identical messages at the murder scenes."

"For my sins," I murmured.

Preston had been listening to the conversation in silence, his gaze moving from Lestrade to Holmes in something of the manner of a spectator at a tennis match. But at that, he frowned. "That is odd. Makes it sound like the work of a religious maniac."

"Or someone pretending to be one," Lestrade put in.

Preston was still frowning at the carpet. "The only maniac who's appeared in the case so far is Sir Galahad. At first glance, it's hard to see what motive he could have had for murdering Huxley, when according to everything we've heard, he was on the point of granting Sir Galahad his loan. But what if I'm right about the Earl of Tottenham having been responsible for the stolen bonds?"

Holmes inclined his head. "A valid question indeed." His expression was still neutral, but I caught that oddly significant undercurrent to his words once again.

"Well, Huxley could have been in on it with him," Preston went on. "And had second thoughts, so he had to be silenced. Or else he discovered the truth about the bonds, and the Earl killed him to stop him talking."

Lestrade looked slightly more cheerful. "That could make sense. And perhaps Mrs. Clair witnessed the crime—or knew too much about Sir Galahad's dealings with Huxley. Then she had to be silenced, too."

I thought that the theory hung together quite well. But Holmes appeared not to be paying attention. He was once more staring out of the window, his expression fixed.

This time, I could not restrain myself from speaking. "I'm sure that Jack and Lucy will return soon, Holmes. And that they will have news of Becky and Flynn."

"You mistake me, Watson." Holmes's gaze didn't waver from the window. "My reason for studying the pavement below us is that in the past half hour, I have observed among the pedestrians a young woman walking a Pekinese dog, an elderly matron with a shopping basket over her arm, and a young man in sailor's garb, apparently something the worse for an evening spent in the grog shops."

"What—" Preston began, frowning.

Holmes held up a hand. "What is significant about the appearance of these personages is that all three have worn identical pairs of boots: brown, with a frayed lace on the right side and a scuff on the left toe."

Lestrade's brows went up. "Meaning that they're all the same person?"

"Such was my conclusion."

Holmes's tone was entirely unconcerned, but I still started up from my chair. "Surely we ought to go out there and—"

"And do what?" Holmes put up a hand to stop me before I could make a move towards the door. "Accuse this individual of walking on a public street? No crime has been committed. Nor do we have any indication that this person is in any way connected to the case we have at hand. Due to the notoriety of your literary endeavors, Watson, quite a number of strange individuals seek out 221B Baker Street out of mere curiosity."

I did not quite believe that explanation. Nor, in my opinion, did Holmes. But by this point in our long association, I was willing to trust in his plans, even when he did not see fit to share them aloud.

I subsided once more into my chair as Holmes added, "Besides, the drunken sailor has disappeared around the corner of Melcombe Street. If he or she returns in another guise, that will be time enough to decide whether we wish to force a confrontation."

There was a moment's silence, and then Preston shifted in his chair. "Is that all you wanted to discuss, Mr. Holmes? If it is, I think I'd better get along. I've a hotel room booked in Tottenham so that I can be on hand to interview the employees at the bank first thing in the morning."

Holmes turned away from the window at last, letting the curtain fall back into place. "Your energy does both you and the Pinkerton's agency credit, Mr. Preston. Yes, I believe that is all for the present. If you will leave Watson with the name and address of your hotel, we shall be sure to communicate with you in case of any further developments."

Mr. Preston was already on his feet. "Thank you, Mr. Holmes, I'm much obliged."

He departed, and Lestrade left soon after, citing the need to write up a report for his superiors at Scotland Yard.

Holmes remained at the window, though he had let the curtain fall back into place enough that only a narrow sliver of glass remained through which he could keep watch on the street below.

"Well, Holmes?" I asked.

"Well, Watson?" There was a brief glimmer of humor in Holmes's gray eyes, but it was mixed with a kind of steely determination. "Did anything strike you about our recent conversation?"

I considered. "For one thing, it strikes me as odd that Mr. Brown wants to return to America so soon, now that he knows that two murders have actually been committed. He gave every sign of being in fear for his daughter's life. If he really mistrusts Sir Galahad and believes him to be plotting to kill her, would he not wish to stay and do everything in his power to protect his daughter? Particularly since you could offer him no assurance of being able to help."

"Yes, his behavior is distinctly odd in that regard. Anything else?" Holmes asked.

"Mr. Preston departed very suddenly. And it seemed to me that although he has appeared to be perfectly open in his dealings with us so far, he was less than forthcoming about his reasons for leaving here in such a hurry."

"Your conclusion?"

"That he either knows or suspects something about the individual who keeps changing costume in order to watch the flat?"

I was not sure that Holmes would answer, but he steepled his fingers, his eyes half-closed. "That was my conclusion, as well. It will be interesting to see what transpires—"

He broke off as the door to the sitting room burst open and Becky and Flynn burst into the room.

Becky was already speaking, her words tumbling out in a rush from the moment her feet crossed the threshold. "Yes, I know we shouldn't have gone off alone, everyone was probably worried and we're very sorry, but before you start scolding us, there are things you need to know!"

Holmes rarely smiled, but I saw his lips give a distinct twitch as he regarded her. "Very well, you may safely consider all recriminations shelved."

Becky had stopped short, looking around the room. "Oh. Are Jack and Lucy not here?"

"No, they went to Tottenham in search of you two, and have

not yet returned. But proceed. What is this vital information which you have to impart?"

Becky took a breath. "We went to Tottenham, too."

"And spent a not-insignificant amount of time underground, it would appear." Holmes regarded the smudges of dirt on both of their clothing.

"Yes. In a root cellar." Becky was speaking only marginally more slowly now. "We were following someone away from Mr. Huxley's house, and we found an empty cottage in the woods. Whoever we were following—at least, we think it was the man we were following—knocked us both out and put us in the root cellar."

"Took us awhile to get out again," Flynn put in.

"Yes. But when we did, we searched the cottage. It was filled with plants and chemistry equipment." Becky waved her hand at Holmes's various beakers and burners arrayed on his worktable. "As though someone were doing experiments, or brewing things. But we also found this."

Digging in her pocket, Becky produced a photograph, which she handed over to Holmes.

"Very interesting." Holmes studied the photograph for a moment, then handed it across to me. I looked down at the faces of two children who appeared to be around the same ages as Becky and Flynn, though dressed in the fashions of more than a decade ago. "Was there anything else?"

"Yes! While we were searching the cottage, we both smelled smoke."

"Someone was burning something," Flynn confirmed. "The smell kept getting stronger."

"Exactly. So we left the cottage and looked around a bit, and we found a spot where someone had made a terrific fire.

Everything was still smoldering, but it looked as though they'd been burning papers, or maybe books."

"Was anything salvageable?" Holmes asked.

Becky shook her head regretfully. "No. It was all still on fire. And we were afraid that whoever had started it burning would come back and try to knock us out and put us down in the root cellar again."

"Or worse," Flynn said. "They'd be chumps to let us escape a second time."

"So we caught the train to London and came back here," Becky said. "Oh! But I nearly forgot. This might be the most important thing of all." She reached into her pocket again, this time coming up with a much-wrinkled sheet of paper. "It's a letter, or the start of one. And we think it's about Mr. Huxley! Here."

She passed the paper across to Holmes, who read it with a furrow between his brows. This time, there was no mistaking the gleam of quickening excitement that appeared beneath his half-veiled eyes.

"How did you come by this?"

Flynn and Becky exchanged a look, and Becky said, "There was a woman. First she came to the house—this morning, after Lucy had gone—and pretended to be taking a census. We knew she was lying about that, so we tried following her, but then we lost her. Only we saw her again in Tottenham, at the castle fair. And then she found us when we were down in the root cellar. She said that she couldn't risk helping us get out, because she couldn't let anyone in the neighborhood know that she'd been there."

"Those were her exact words?" Holmes said.

Becky and Flynn exchanged another look, and then Flynn said, "Pretty close. Far as I can remember, she said the stakes were higher than we knew, and that she couldn't risk anyone suspecting her. Sounded to me like she'd already been visiting someone nearby—Sir Galahad up at the castle, maybe—in disguise, and didn't want her cover getting blown."

Becky nodded agreement. "She said she would send help back for us if we couldn't get out ourselves. And then she tossed a parcel of food down to us. And that"—she nodded to the unfinished letter Holmes held—"was wrapped around one of the sandwiches."

Holmes's brows edged up a fraction of an inch. "A unique method of passing information, and one which explains the traces of cheese and pickle which are visible at the paper's edges. And our mystery woman said nothing more?"

Flynn and Becky both shook their heads. "Nothing."

"Well, you have both done excellently. And I hardly need add that we are relieved to have you returned, none the worse for your misadventures. Now, if you would like to visit Mrs. Hudson in the kitchen, I'm sure that she would be happy to procure some supper for you."

The two of them started for the door, although Becky paused halfway. "What about Lucy and Jack?"

"You need have no fears on that score. Assuming that they are still in Tottenham, I plan to telephone to them directly, both to apprise them of your safe return and to make a request or two as to their next move."

Becky's expression betrayed a lively curiosity as to what those requests might be, but she started to follow Flynn out the door without asking any more questions. Possibly because she was too relieved to have avoided remonstrance for having gone to Tottenham without notice.

"Oh." Becky stopped, though, just as she reached the door. "I forgot to give you this."

She drew a small metal object from her pocket and held it out to Holmes.

"Flynn managed to dig that out of the fire we were telling you about." She nodded to the object in Holmes's hand. "We think it's a key."

Holmes held the metal object between his thumb and forefinger, and I saw his posture stiffen perceptibly as he studied it.

But he said only, "Thank you. We shall return to Galahad's castle in the morning, and can investigate the scene of the fire more fully then."

Becky nodded and went out, her light footsteps pattering back down the stairs to the kitchen.

Holmes returned to his study of the key.

"What does it mean, Holmes?" I ventured at last.

Holmes cast a quick, frowning glance up at me. "I believe, Watson, that it means my suspicions are about to be confirmed."

"Who do you think the woman—" I began.

Holmes held up a hand. "I will be happy to discuss that with you at a later time, but for now, I had better make good on my promise to reach Lucy and Jack by telephone if at all possible."

Chapter 24: Lucy

I had to give Nibbs credit; he had immersed himself thoroughly in his assigned part. If Sir Galahad gave the impression of a man playing the stage role of a medieval lord, then Nibbs could easily be taking part in a theatrical performance, as well—this one set several centuries later and involving masked highwaymen.

Nibbs had forgone his usual tattered hodgepodge of clothing in favor of black from head to toe: black overcoat, black trousers and boots. He had even, despite the short notice, found a black mask that covered the entire upper half of his face, and had blackened his jaw and chin to match with what looked like boot polish.

To anyone who knew him, the effect might be more comical than sinister—particularly when he took off the mask—but anyone caught off guard would find him an impressive figure. Lady Carlotta drew back with a gasp of alarm, and her husband startled and stared.

"Did he take anything?"

"I don't know." Jack kept a firm hold on the back of Nibbs' coat collar. "I didn't find anything on him, but you'd probably do well to take a quick inventory of anything valuable you have on the premises here, just in case he had an accomplice who's already gotten away."

"Yes—yes, of course." For the first time since my arrival at the castle, Sir Galahad looked genuinely shaken at the reality that had just intruded on his happy Arthurian daydream. "Apart from the castle itself, really the only valuables we have here are in the artifact room, and that's always kept locked. But we'd better make sure."

The door opened once again to admit a dark-haired man with a friendly, clean-shaven face. Unlike Sir Galahad and his knights, he wore ordinary, modern-day clothes: a black dinner jacket and tie. He carried a leather-bound book under one arm, and pushed up the wire-rimmed pair of spectacles that had slid down the bridge of his nose before speaking.

"Good evening, all. Sorry I'm late, I found an interesting annotation in an early edition of Bede's chronicles—" he stopped, catching sight of Jack and Nibbs. "I say, is something wrong?"

Sir Galahad rallied from his shock enough to answer. "Ah. Merlin. I'm glad you're here. Yes, this is Sergeant Kelly from Scotland Yard. He just caught this vile ruffian trying to break into the castle. I was just about to show him to the artifacts room so that we can make sure that nothing has been stolen."

Jack's eyes met mine over the top of Nibbs' head. We had decided before coming to the castle that it would be better for the sake of the investigation if we pretended to be strangers to one another, which limited the degree to which we could openly communicate. But I caught the message in Jack's gaze all the same and stepped forward.

"I could help with that. I'm sure you want to get done as quickly as possible, in case anything has been taken and you need to take steps to find this burglar's accomplices. Maybe you, Sir Galahad, could show Sergeant Kelly over the rest of the castle to look for any other signs of forced entry? And your friend—Merlin, was it?—and I could visit the artifacts room."

I watched Sir Galahad closely to see how he would respond, but he nodded without any apparent hesitation. "An admirable suggestion, thank you, Miss James. Merlin knows the collection as well as I do myself." He turned to Jack. "Sergeant Kelly, we can safely leave the miscreant in the dungeon with my knights on guard while we make our search. I assure you they will not allow him to escape."

At the mention of a dungeon, Nibbs' eyes widened and he cast a swift and dirty glance at Jack. I mentally added several pounds to the fee we would end up paying him when all of this was over, but at least he said nothing.

"Thank you, Sir Galahad," Jack said. "You can lead the way."

* * *

"Have you known Sir Galahad for long?" I asked.

Peter Calloway—maybe it was the modern clothes, but I was having a difficult time thinking of him as Merlin—and I were in the artifacts room, which proved to be a small chamber off the main hall of the castle. The stone walls were covered in reproduction tapestries, interspersed with wooden racks that held an array of gleaming swords and axes. Glass display cases shone with highly polished golden cups and chalices and a few pieces of medieval jewelry: rings and wristlets and a heavy golden necklace inlaid with rubies.

In answer to my question, Peter glanced up from the dagger that he'd been replacing on the velvet bed of its display case.

"Oh, for years, now. Ever since we were at school together. My family's American, but my father sent me over to here to Cambridge to study. I think he hoped I'd go in for something like law or medicine. But I caught the Medieval bug when I was in my first year, and after that it was all over." He clicked the display case closed, locked it, and smiled. "Too late to get me interested in anything else."

I nodded, although the truth was that I was struggling to focus on the conversation. Sir Galahad's willingness to let Jack search the premises could mean that Becky and Flynn were here, but he himself was unaware of that fact. Or it could mean that they were so well hidden that he was entirely confident that a search wouldn't reveal their presence.

Or he might have acquiesced to the search because he knew quite well that they weren't here at all.

None of the three options was particularly encouraging. But I was here with Galahad's closest friend, who seemed perfectly agreeable to answering questions. It wouldn't do Flynn and Becky any good if I wasted the opportunity.

"Is that how you and Sir Galahad met?" I asked. "Over your shared love of history?"

Peter leaned forwards a little across one of the display cases. "Look here, I'm sure this must seem like a completely crazy setup to you, Miss James. Grown men dressing up and playing at knights like a lot of ten-year-old kids. But Galahad's a good sort, really. Generous to a fault, and loyal. He sees the evils of our modern age, and wants to combat them with a return to simpler times. Is that an unworthy goal?"

It was debatable whether life really had been simpler in the days of knights and feudal lords—or any more pleasant for the average man or woman. But I asked, "And you? Do you share Sir Galahad's goal of a return to courtly living?"

"Me?" Peter's smile was frank and engaging. "I'll be honest with you. My goal after leaving school was to find a position as a history professor on the faculty of some college or university. Those types of jobs proving scarce as the proverbial hens' teeth, I was happy—overjoyed, in fact—to accept Galahad's offer to allow me to live here, oversee his excavations, and continue my own scholarly research."

I looked around the room. "And all of these artifacts were dug up on the grounds of the castle here?"

"Well." Peter coughed, looking momentarily embarrassed, then smiled again. "So long as I'm being honest, no. None of them were actually dug up here. The best we've been able to find are some broken bits of pottery and a horseshoe that probably wasn't more than a century or so old. Galahad purchased these." He indicated the hanging weapons and the display cases all around. "But it makes for a better story if he can claim that they're part of the castle's history. And if there's one thing you should know about Galahad, it's that he'll always choose a good story over an inconvenient truth."

"Did you know Lady Carlotta before her marriage to Sir Galahad?" I asked.

"Carlotta?" Peter looked surprised. "Oh, because we're both American? No. Let's just say that her family moved in very different circles from mine."

His manner was as affable as before, but there was a note of reserve in his voice that made me look at him more closely.

"You didn't approve of Sir Galahad's marrying her?"

"Look here, I didn't say that." Peter gave an awkward shrug. "She's all right. A bit of a wet blanket, but then it takes a rare woman to put up with all of Galahad's quirks and foibles. She manages pretty well, all things considered."

"What about Rose, his first wife?"

"Rose?" Peter's lips pursed in a silent whistle. "Now, she was a handful—a real she-devil when she wanted to be. Hated it here, hated everything about the castle, and wasn't shy about making her feelings known. She led poor Galahad a merry dance. But he was heartbroken when she died, so I suppose the poor sap must have loved her all the same."

The door to the artifacts room opened, and one of Galahad's knights—the same man who had poured our tea—put his head in.

"Telephone call for yer, Miss James," he grunted.

Chapter 25: Violet

"Two meetings in as many days." One of Preston's brows was elevated. "What did I do to get so lucky?"

The Oriental tea shop was closed at this hour, but he'd found her, nonetheless. Not that she'd made it particularly difficult. After turning off of Baker Street, she'd found a small square of green park and had taken up a position on a stone bench that stood beneath a cherry tree. She'd had to fend off three propositions from men who took her for a lady of the evening before Preston's arrival, but it made for a good spot from which to keep watch on the road and the passing traffic.

Ordinarily, she would have taken it as a point of pride to find a suitably sarcastic or insulting response to Preston's greeting. But tonight, she said only, "There are two children locked in the cellar of a cottage on the Trent estate in Tottenham. I would have gotten them out, but I'd just been there that afternoon—barely half an hour before I found them—paying a call on the cottage's tenant. I couldn't risk him beginning to suspect that my visit wasn't for the reasons I'd claimed."

Preston slid onto the bench beside her. "Pretending to be a newspaper reporter again?"

She shrugged. "It's a fairly good cover. One of the few occupations open to women, and people expect reporters to ask a lot of questions. Not to mention, most people are so thrilled at the idea of having their name in the newspaper that they're more than willing to answer those questions."

"Everyone wants to be famous," Preston agreed. "Unless they're a criminal."

Violet thought there might be a case for criminals being the most eager for fame of all. But she didn't have the capacity for a philosophical discussion just now. She'd had nothing to eat all day; the heat of the railway journey back to town had given her a headache—and she was beginning to doubt her decision to leave the children in the cellar.

She'd been afraid at the time that freeing them would not only ruin her cover but allow a murderer to escape before the evidence against him could be found. That was the goal of every investigation she undertook: to ensure that justice was done.

There'd been so many times when she was growing up that she'd been helpless to do anything but watch while the innocent suffered and the guilty got off scot-free. She'd sworn from the moment she was hired at Pinkerton's never to let that happen again.

But now, weighed against the possible threat to two children's lives, even justice seemed like a paltry reason for having walked away.

"The children," she said. "They work for Mr. Holmes, or I'm fairly certain that they do. I did try to point his daughter in the right direction when I saw her at the train station. But if they've not been found yet, someone needs to go and get them out of the cellar. Unless they've already managed to escape. They seemed like a resourceful pair."

"Blond-haired boy and girl, both about eleven years old?"

"Yes?"

Preston stretched out his long legs, crossing them at the

ankles. "You can rest easy on that score. When I left Mr. Holmes, they were just coming up the street, heading for 221B."

Violet released a breath, surprised by the strength of the relief she felt. She'd always prided herself on not allowing sentimentality to cloud her judgment or interfere with her investigations.

"Good."

Preston gave her a searching look, which made her cheeks heat up. Wonderful. Now Preston had caught her behaving like a milksop.

"Feeling grateful enough to tell me who you're working for?" he asked.

"Very funny. I thought we'd already covered that one."

"What about telling me who lives in this cottage you visited?" Preson asked.

Violet debated. But he could find out the answer for himself easily enough. And whatever her own personal feelings in the matter, she had to admit that he would probably be more useful to her as an ally than an enemy.

Or if not an ally, at least she could avoid deliberately antagonizing him.

"A man called Peter Calloway. He's a close friend of Sir Galahad's from their school days."

Preston looked at her with quickening interest. "Meaning that he's someone who might know about any skeletons lurking in the Earl's closet?"

"That's what I was hoping for, yes."

"Any luck?"

"That depends," Violet said.

"On?"

"On how much information you're willing to share in return."

She would have sworn that a corner of Preston's mouth twitched in brief amusement. But then he gave her a long look, clearly running through the facts of the case in his own mind. Probably trying to select the least helpful fact he could think to offer her.

On the opposite side of the park, a beggar boy on crutches was approaching passers-by, whining for coins to help a poor cripple. Although Violet strongly suspected that if you took away the crutches, he'd be able to walk just fine.

Preston watched the boy approach a fat man in a top hat. Then at last he said, "There's some talk about the death of Sir Galahad's first wife."

Violet brushed that aside. "Yes, I know. She fell off one of the castle towers. Or was pushed. Peter Calloway—or Merlin, as he's known locally—told me all about it today."

Preston looked alert. "Did he?"

"Yes." Violet paused, choosing her words carefully. "He said several times that Sir Galahad was absolutely devastated by her death, and that if anyone claimed that he'd had something to do with the accident, they were utterly wrong."

"Ah. Said it so often, in fact, that the impression conveyed was the exact opposite?"

"You could say that. Your turn."

Preston frowned, but surprisingly didn't object to being asked to share. "Sir Galahad has quite a reputation among the locals around the castle. Part respect, part fear."

"How so?"

"He and his knights, as he calls them, have a reputation for executing a kind of vigilante justice on anyone they judge guilty of behaving disrespectfully towards women. Actually, I'm not sure the knights he's hired care much about the disrespectful part as they do about getting to bash someone repeatedly."

"Really." Violet hadn't heard that. "Well, I suppose if that's true, they're probably closer to the real King Arthur than any of the ridiculous legends that we have today."

"How's that?"

"The real King Arthur—if he existed at all, that is—wasn't a king; he was a sixth century war lord who fought back against the Saxon invasion of Britain during a particularly nasty and brutal time in English history. He'd probably have laughed himself sick at all the fair flower of English chivalry nonsense that got heaped on later—heaped on by the French, too, mostly. It was the French troubadours who started spreading all the round-table stories centuries later."

Violet stopped. Preston was looking at her with a mixture of surprise and curiosity that made her face flush again.

"My grandfather was a professor of Medieval Literature at Harvard. I spent a summer with him before he died."

The happiest summer of her life to that point, but Preston definitely didn't need to know that.

Preston studied her for an uncomfortable moment longer—which made her wonder how much he was guessing, despite everything that she hadn't actually said. His face, as usual, betrayed nothing of his thoughts, and after a second or two, he let it go.

"So the question is whether Sir Galahad could have gotten it into his head that Mr. Huxley was behaving disrespectfully towards a woman—or women." He frowned. "His assistant at the bank was female. I'd wonder if there was anything there, but for one thing she was about a hundred, and for another, she was murdered, too, in the same way that Huxley was."

Violet hesitated. But she'd already sent the information along to Mr. Holmes by way of the children. In the moment, it had been a sop for her conscience at having left them imprisoned. And if what Preston had told her was true, they were probably handing over the half-finished letter she'd found to Mr. Holmes right now.

"There might have been something," she said. "I did go to Mrs. Claire's house. I had a look through the bins outside." She'd looked through Mr. Huxley's, too, before his harridan of a housekeeper had interrupted her, but she hadn't found anything at Huxley's that had been nearly as interesting. "I found a half-finished letter that she'd been writing to her sister, from the sound of it. She mentioned being very upset by some rumours that she'd heard about Mr. Huxley."

"I see." Preston's gaze unfocused briefly. It was fully dark now, but the orange glow of a nearby street lamp threw his face into harsh planes of light and shadow. He was silent for a long moment—long enough for Violet to wonder again what he was thinking. Then he said, "Sir Galahad's pretty well broke. Hence the loan he was trying to get from Huxley. But his property's sitting on land with some valuable mineral rights attached to it. He doesn't want to dig up the property or sell to any mining outfits, since that'd mean scrapping all his King-Arthur-in-his-castle stuff. But he was trying to use the rights as security for the bank loan."

Ah. Violet felt a prickle, three parts annoyance, one part even more irritating pleasure, at the fact that Preston's thoughts had been running along the same lines as hers. She was used to working through a case, developing her theories entirely on her own, and it was surprisingly … nice to, for once, be talking through the facts with someone else. Or it would have been, if that someone else hadn't been the man sitting beside her.

She should have known he'd reach a similar conclusion, though—and quickly, at that. Preston was many things, but even she had to admit he was an excellent detective.

"I'm planning to be at the grand opening ceremony at the castle tomorrow," she said. "What about you?"

Preston quirked up an eyebrow. "Are you actually suggesting we go in on this together?"

Violet shrugged. "There's a first time for everything."

Chapter 26: Lucy

The train station was nearly deserted at this hour of the night, which made it easy to spot Nibbs and Jack. They were sitting on one of the covered benches that lined the platform. Nibbs was still in handcuffs, and—predictably—was grumbling about it.

"I don't see why you can't unlock these blasted things." He gave the chain between his wrists a shake. "Cursed uncomfortable, they are."

Jack didn't bother to move. "Right. Or I could just go back to Galahad's castle, knock on the door, and tell Sir Galahad that your attempt to break in was all a fake. That would have about the same effect."

Nibbs gave Jack a mournful look. "That's all very well for you to say, Sergeant. You're not the one getting paraded about in ruffles. I've got my reputation to think about, you know."

"Your reputation," Jack said. "Right. If there were a Madame Tussaud's gallery of thieves—"

"Think I'd be in it?" Nibbs asked with a sudden hint of pride in his tone.

"No, I think every man, woman, and child who walked into it would come out with empty pockets, because you would have picked off all their valuables while they were looking around."

Nibbs looked aggrieved. I hid a smile and quickened my pace to join them. In order to keep up the pretense of being strangers to one another, we'd had to leave Galahad's Castle separately, which meant that I hadn't yet had the chance to tell Jack about my telephone call with Holmes.

"Ah, if it isn't Mrs. Sergeant." Nibbs mournfully reproachful expression changed to one of equally lugubrious appeal at the sight of me. "I was just telling your husband here about the cruel treatment I got from those men up at the castle. Knocked me about something terrible, they did, after they'd hauled me off to the dungeon."

Since he didn't appear to be in the slightest degree injured, I took that claim with a grain of salt.

"Did you notice anything of interest about them, while they were guarding you? Or overhear anything they said?"

"Well, now." Nibbs scratched his chin, which was still covered in boot polish. "Seems to me like maybe I did hear them talking a bit. But I can't remember for the moment what they said."

"And let me guess, I suppose that nothing but an addition to your fee for tonight's performance will jog your memory?"

I'd long ago decided that Nibbs was fundamentally incapable of feeling either shame or embarrassment. His eyes widened as though struck by the novelty of that idea.

"Now that you mention it, I believe an extra spot of the needful wouldn't hurt. Very kind of you to offer."

I dug into my pocketbook and produced a five-shilling piece.

Nibbs opened his mouth, doubtless to demand more, if past experience with him held true.

Jack looked at him sideways. "Before you ask for any more, let me remind you that I'm the one paying your fare back to London, and that I could just forget about it and leave you here.

And while we're talking memory troubles, I could always forget where I put the key to your handcuffs."

Nibbs heaved a deep sigh, but held his cuffed hands out for the five shillings. "Fine, fine, have it your own way. Can't tell you much about those knights of Sir Galahad's anyway. All I really overheard was them talking about the big ceremony tomorrow—asking each other what else needed to be done, that kind of thing."

"I don't suppose you recognized any of them?" Jack asked. "Any well-known pinchers or St. Nicholas clerks among them?"

Both of those were terms for London street thieves, I knew, although I wasn't entirely sure of the varieties. London's underworld was divided into categories as specialized as the departments in an academic institution. Some stole jewelry, some picked pockets, some robbed the chronic drunkards as they left the gin halls and pubs …

Nibs, though, gave a brief, scornful snort. "Nah. None of them's that sort. Lot of honest blokes, as far as I could see. Doubt any of 'em had ever gotten so much as a tail piece in the steel."

* * *

"Tail piece in the steel?" I asked Jack.

We had given Nibbs his payment for tonight's work and loaded him—unhandcuffed at the last moment—onto a train going back to town. Now we were walking a short distance along darkened streets to the small traveler's inn near the station.

"Three months' prison sentence," Jack said. "According to Nibbs, none of Sir Galahad's knights is the type to have done time."

"That's interesting." It was a surprise, given the knights' general air of menace. But I didn't doubt Nibbs' ability to distinguish an honest man from a dishonest one at first glance. He'd spent his entire life among the criminal classes after all.

"What did your father say on the telephone?" Jack asked. "And why are we suddenly spending the night here?"

"First of all, Becky and Flynn are with Holmes now," I said. "Apparently, they had one of their usual hair-raising escapades after deciding to look into Mr. Huxley's murder for themselves, but they're back in Baker Street, safe and sound. And second, we're staying here because Holmes wants us to find an excuse to go up to the castle again tomorrow. You can either ask more questions about Mr. Huxley or else claim that you're still investigating Nibbs' attempted robbery, and I'm supposed to engage Lady Carlotta in conversation so that I can ask her a question."

Jack's brows crept upwards. "What question would that be?"

"Holmes wants to know whether she's heard of any derogatory rumours about Mr. Huxley circulating around the community here."

"Rumours?"

"Yes. According to Holmes, the answer should be 'instructive.'"

CHAPTER 27: VIOLET

Violet pushed aside the screen of maple branches and stepped into the clearing. The summer sun was shining, the birds were singing, and yet the cottage looked somehow even more eerie and sinister than it had in the twilight the night before. The light exposed the barren patches in the roof thatch, the cracks in the whitewashed walls—and closely fitting shutters that covered every square inch of the windows and were by far in the best state of repair out of anything about the entire building.

It might have been Violet's on-edge nerves—or memories of other similarly isolated places she'd been—but the entire place seemed to fairly scream that it had morbid secrets to keep.

Well, she wasn't going to learn any of those secrets by standing out here. She took a step forward …

The unmistakable sound of a revolver being cocked clicked in the trees behind her, and a deep voice drawled, "Run and you'll die tired."

The fact that she recognized the voice stopped her heart from leaping out of her chest, but did nothing for the punch of anger at herself that hit her in the gut. She hadn't suspected for a moment that she wasn't alone out here; hadn't even heard him coming.

To be safe, she put up her hands. From the sound of his voice, he was still a good fifty feet away, but underestimating Preston's marksmanship was like going over Niagara Falls in a barrel. No good reason to do it unless you were prepared to die.

"Turn around. Slowly," Preston said.

She did as she was told, only because the extra time she took gave her a chance to compose her expression into one of calm before facing him.

She arched an eyebrow. "I thought we agreed to meet at the fairgrounds in an hour."

If he'd gotten the drop on her, she at least had the small satisfaction of seeing his jaw unhinge briefly, as shocked recognition flared in his gaze.

In Preston's defense, she'd dressed for this expedition in a man's riding kit: coat and breeches, and her hair twisted up under a helmet. Padding in the coat made her shoulders look wider than they really were, and prosthetics in her cheeks changed the shape of her jawline to appear more male. From a distance—to anyone's eyes but Preston's—she'd look like a country squire, out for a morning ride.

Preston's gaze narrowed briefly before returning to his usual wry good-humor. Now that she thought of it, his near-constant air of easy-going affability was very much like the shutters on the cottage: just as calculated and controlled; just as effective at keeping his private thoughts in and other people out.

"You didn't tell me you were planning to come here first," he said.

Violet spat the cheek prosthetics out—they were incredibly uncomfortable—and tucked them into her pocket before replying. "For that, I would have had to trust you, and unfortunately I don't. With good reason, apparently."

Preston's lazy grin acknowledged the fact that he'd also

planned a lone visit to the cottage this morning, without informing her of the fact.

He slid the revolver he'd been leveling at her back into the holster he wore under his arm. "Well, now that we're both here, what's say we have a look around?"

Violet eyed the cottage. "I'm not sure that's a good idea."

Preston gave her another slow grin. "Not scared, are you?"

"What are you, six?" Actually, she could just picture Preston at six years old. He'd probably looked like a blue-eyed little angel, and been the holy terror of all the other children on the school playground.

Preston started for the cottage door, moving with the loose, easy stride that always made her think of a mountain lion: relaxed and yet predatory, deceptively casual, but able to cover ground as rapidly as a run.

Since the alternative was letting him search the place alone, Violet followed, pausing in the doorway to let her eyes adjust to the dim light.

The interior looked almost exactly the same as it had when she'd called here yesterday. Sparsely furnished, with only a couple of rough wooden chairs near the hearth, and the rest of the space taken up by worktables, baskets, and shelves.

Only a few of the baskets of herbs and beakers for chemicals were ever so slightly out of place from where they'd been. If it had been Holmes's two child associates who'd searched the place, they'd done a near-professional job of keeping the signs of their investigation to a minimum.

Preston stood in the center of the floor, thumbs in his pockets, his expression still lazy, but his eyes sharp, ticking off points of potential interest.

His gaze focused on the chemistry apparatus spread out across the worktable at the back of the room near the hearth. "Looks like the setup my granddad used for making his homemade moonshine. Any idea what—"

Something creaked and rustled above their heads, and he broke off, tilting his head up and frowning. "Sounds like something's up there on the roof."

Violet listened, but the sound didn't come again. "A squirrel, maybe? Or a raccoon?"

Preston's gaze was still on the low beamed ceiling above them. "Do they have 'coons over here in England?"

Come to think of it, Violet had no idea. She'd already been surprised to find that the squirrels here were red-brown, not gray. But she was beginning to get a crawling, uneasy feeling about being here, and she'd been in this game long enough to listen to those kinds of instincts.

"We should finish looking around and get out," she started to say.

Something crashed down through the chimney and exploded in the fireplace in a shower of sparks, gushing liquid, and broken glass. Rivers of fire spread out from the fireplace with seemingly impossible quickness, licking the wooden floorboards, spreading to the reed baskets of dried plants and herbs, which crackled, caught fire, and burst into flame like so many safety matches.

For an instant or two, Violet could only stand gaping, her sluggish brain unable to entirely process what had just happened—although once her nostrils had caught the sharp smell of what she guessed was turpentine, she had a better idea.

"Bottle filled with something flammable and stuffed with a burning rag," Preston said grimly. "I've seen them used in

New York and Chicago when the street gangs are at war with each other."

Violet had, too. And this overcrowded cottage might have been specially designed to go up in smoke the moment the fire touched it. She jumped back, beating at a spark that had leaped from one of the baskets to her breeches.

Preston was making for one of the windows, so she crossed to the door instead, lifting the latch and shoving hard.

Her stomach dropped. "It's locked!"

Preston turned. "What do you mean?"

"Do I have to define locked for you?" Violet snapped. A cold, unfriendly fist was trying to close around her heart. "What about the windows?"

Preston tried to push up the sash on the nearest one. The muscles of his back and shoulders stood out beneath the fabric of his shirt, but he finally gave up with a shake of his head. "Must be nailed shut."

"Nailed shut? Who nails shut their windows?"

"Someone who doesn't want any intruders getting in."

Or someone constructing a nice tight trap. Which she and Preston had just walked straight into.

"This is your fault!"

Preston gave her a quirked-up eyebrow. "My fault? How d'you figure?"

"You're the one who insisted on coming in here."

And she was the one who'd been idiot enough to respond to his taunting and follow him, but she was ignoring that fact for now.

The fire had already raced along the work table and around the perimeter of the room, penning in them into the small square of floor in the center.

GALAHAD'S CASTLE 175

Preston stamped out another spark that had jumped across the floor. "What's say we postpone the faultfinding until we're certain we're going to get out of this alive, shall we?"

"Fine." Violet looked at the walls around them, which were alive with flames. The air was hot and growing thick with smoke, stinging her eyes, burning the back of her throat. "You have a gun. Why don't you try shooting through the fastenings on the window?"

"That's a last resort." Preston still sounded calm, which infuriated her even more. "Firing off a shot in an enclosed space like this—you're risking the bullet's ricocheting and hitting you."

"I think I'd take my chances–" Violet started to say.

An entire section of the roof above their heads collapsed. Violet had a heart-stopping split-second to see the beams and the thatched straw falling, but no time to react or jump out of the way.

A wooden beam struck the side of her head and her vision went black.

CHAPTER 28: WATSON

"I cannot possibly do that, Mr. Holmes."

"I think you can, Mr. Sherwood," Holmes replied.

We were back at the Tottenham Bank, and once again in the office of Mr. Sherwood. The bank president appeared even more worried and uncomfortable than he had at our last meeting.

"Not without the consent of the deposit box owner." Sherwood's mustache quivered and his blue eyes flashed with determination.

"Or without a search warrant," Holmes replied, in that calm, silken tone that he sometimes employs when he knows he has the upper hand. "Which we can readily obtain, and then, with the police, open the box for ourselves."

"On what grounds?"

"Seeking the warrant, I will argue before the magistrate that the contents of the box are directly connected with Huxley's murder. My argument will become part of the public record. You can allow that to happen, or you can examine the contents of the box for yourself and tell me what is there. I do not need to be present."

"I need two keys to open the box."

"Quite right. You have the bank's key. Here is the other."

So saying, he took a key from his waistcoat pocket and handed it over. Sherwood held it between his thumb and forefinger.

From his expression of distaste, the key might have been a wriggling worm taken from a compost heap.

"How did you get this?"

"Quite lawfully, I assure you."

"I don't know that I can rely on your assurances, Mr. Holmes."

Holmes shrugged. "Very well. Come, Watson. The Magistrate's office should be open soon. We shall meet there with Inspector Lestrade. Perhaps some gentlemen of the press will be there as well."

He stood.

Sherwood coughed. "Hang it all, Mr. Holmes, there's no need to be hasty. It's just that I've never been involved with Galahad's box; Huxley did all that. I don't know what to expect to find there. It could prove embarrassing for the bank, if there's …"

He trailed off and made a show of examining his fingertips.

"You are about to say it could embarrass the bank if stolen bearer bonds are found in the box," said Holmes.

Sherwood nodded. "That fellow from Pinkerton's alleged as much."

"Yes, I know. I also have spoken about the matter with Galahad's solicitors, who inspected the bonds that made up the dowry of his wife. They say those bonds were perfectly legitimate. Railroad bonds, Carnegie Steel, and Standard Oil. They also said they had made an inventory book for their client, to be kept in the deposit box, so that annotations could be made as the coupons from the bonds were redeemed."

"Oh." Sherwood appeared considerably relieved. "So that is what I can expect to find?"

"I did not say that, Mr. Sherwood."

"Well, hang it all, what do you expect me to find?"

Holmes took a small white envelope from the inside pocket of his jacket. "I have written that out on a piece of paper and placed it in this envelope. I am fairly confident in my conclusions, but I do need you to confirm that they are correct. Now, will you kindly go to your vault, open Galahad's safe deposit box, and observe the contents? Watson and I will wait for you."

Holmes placed the small envelope on Sherwood's desk.

"You can open this when you return," he said. "Otherwise, I shall trouble you for the key, Watson and I will proceed to visit the magistrate, and the chips, so to speak, will fall where they may."

Sherwood got to his feet and strode from the room without a word.

Holmes and I waited. The clock on his office wall ticked away the minutes. Exactly four had elapsed when Sherwood returned. His complexion was ashen.

With shaking fingers, Sherwood picked up the envelope and tore it open. He unfolded the note, glanced at it, and dropped it as if it had scorched his fingers.

"How the devil did you know?" he asked.

"It is my business to know things," said Sherlock Holmes. "Come, Watson."

As we stood, I saw the opened paper on the desk. I read four words, written in Holmes's forceful handwriting:

Galahad's box is empty.

Chapter 29: Lucy

"Yes?" There was a hint of, if not outright impatience, at least abstraction in Sir Galahad's tone as he regarded me over the breakfast table. "You have some further questions to ask?"

He and Lady Carlotta were breakfasting early this morning, in order to be ready for the grand ceremony that would occur later on. He was already dressed in full medieval garb, but Carlotta had forgone historical authenticity in favor of a light floral wrapper and satin slippers.

She looked pale, with shadows under her eyes as though she hadn't slept well, and the bread and cheese on her plate had scarcely been touched.

"I hope it won't take long," I told Sir Galahad. "I know you must have a great deal to do. And it was really more a question for your wife that I wanted to ask."

"For Lottie?" Sir Galahad's brows drew together, and Lady Carlotta gave a small jump of surprise and passed her tongue nervously over her lips.

"For me?"

"Yes. I know you said yesterday that Mr. Huxley didn't seem particularly worried during your meeting. But I was wondering whether you might have heard any rumours circulating about him?"

"Rumours?" Lady Carlotta swallowed. "What do you mean?"

"Any kind of gossip or talk that might be going around to

discredit Mr. Huxley. Anything you might have heard that would diminish his public character."

"No, I don't ..." Lady Carlotta's voice trailed off. "That is, I mean, at least ..."

"At least?" I finally prompted.

Lady Carlotta gave a quick, nervous glance across the table to where her husband sat, then said, her voice scarcely above a whisper. "I had heard ... stories."

"What sort of stories?"

Carlotta looked still more uncomfortable. "I ... well, I may as well tell you. I don't see how it can have anything to do with Mr. Huxley's death. But I knew there had been rumours about him. And I'd learned that the rumours included me. And Galahad's Castle!"

Galahad came to attention at that, setting down his fork with a clatter. "Really, Lottie? You?"

Carlotta was looking down at her own hands, but I saw her flinch at her husband's tone. "Yes. Someone was spreading the rumour that Huxley wanted, well, that he wanted to be my 'perfect gentle knight,' if you know what I mean, and that he would block the loan application for Galahad's Castle until I, well, cooperated."

"I don't believe it!" Galahad's expression was thunderous.

"Of course not!" Carlotta looked up at me, wide-eyed. "And I need hardly say that there wasn't a word of truth in the rumours! Poor Mr. Huxley never asked me for anything at all!"

"How did you hear about the rumour?"

"I was in town doing some shopping the other day. I'd stopped for lunch at the tearoom in the high street, and a woman came up to my table and spoke to me. Quite an elderly, grandmotherly sort of person. But she said that she was from the bank, and that she'd heard an upsetting rumour about Mr. Huxley and me. She'd come to ask me if it was true, because if it was, she would have to tell the bank management and get Mr. Huxley fired."

"Was the woman's name Mrs. Clair?"

"I think so." Carlotta frowned. "I can't remember for certain, but I think that was the name that she gave."

"And did she know who started these rumours?"

Carlotta shook her head. "She didn't say. But after I'd told her that the rumour wasn't in the slightest bit true, she said she was very glad to hear it, because Mr. Huxley was her boss and she liked him."

"When was this?"

"It was a few days ago. Maybe Tuesday? Yes, the day before Daddy and I saw Huxley."

Sir Galahad might have spoken, but the door to the room opened and a burly man whom I recognized as one of his knights put his head in.

"Sorry to interrupt, yer lordship, but we can't find the streamers for the jousting match."

With an exclamation of annoyance, Sir Galahad rose from his chair and followed his retainer out. And since there was no telling when he might return, I leaned forwards and spoke hurriedly and in an undertone to Lady Carlotta.

"This may be a difficult question for you to answer—or even to consider. But I know your husband has strong views on the subject of chivalry. I've heard that at times he even takes punishing men who may have harmed a woman into his own hands."

Lady Carlotta pushed the untasted food around her plate. "Yes. That's true. He wants to bring back the golden age of King

Arthur, you see." Her mouth twisted and her tone was almost bitter as she added, "The days of old when knights were bold. They have the *bold* part right, if nothing else."

"What about his friend Merlin?" I asked. "Does he share your husband's aims?"

"Merlin?" Surprise replaced nervousness on Lady Carlotta's face. "Oh no. That is, I don't believe Merlin pays very much attention to anything except his dusty old books and his gardens. He hardly ever leaves the castle grounds, even, or goes into town to speak to anyone besides Galahad."

"Your husband could have heard the rumours about Mr. Huxley, though. What do you think his reaction might have been if he'd heard the rumours about you and Mr. Huxley?"

Carlotta's throat contracted as she swallowed once again, and she looked down at her own folded hands. When she spoke, it was in scarcely a whisper. "He would have been angry—terribly, terribly angry. Oh, but Galahad cannot have killed Mr. Huxley himself—he would never commit outright murder, and besides, it would have been impossible. Why, he was here at the castle all of that day and night."

"You're certain of that?"

"Why, yes." Lady Carlotta's eyes opened wide. "That is, I think so. Perhaps we weren't together every single moment, but—oh, the idea is too terrible for words! Galahad might believe in a rougher kind of justice than the law provides. But he would never have done such an awful thing. It's only that ..."

"Only that?"

"His knights. Or those dreadful ruffians that he calls his knights." Lady Carlotta gave a small, expressive shiver. "They frighten me sometimes. They'll do anything that Galahad tells them. If they'd heard the rumours about Mr. Huxley—or if Galahad heard the rumours and ordered them to punish Mr. Huxley for behaving dishonorably. Well." Carlotta stopped and looked up at me with appeal in her gaze. "I cannot believe that Galahad would have condoned murder. But it is possible that his knights might have misunderstood—or else gotten carried away and gone too far."

Chapter 30: Watson

Two guards stepped back and swung open the two tall wrought-iron gates at the front entrance to Galahad's Castle. A crowd of villagers and sightseers surged forward, heading down the long, gravel drive that ran straight through the park-like lawn, all the way to the castle tower.

Holmes and I entered with the crowd. His sharp grey eyes glittered as he scanned the faces of those around us. I watched, hoping to spot what he was looking for. Excited children tugged at the sleeves of harried parents. Middle-aged matrons clutched the arms of reluctant husbands. A few men had their coats draped over their arms, even though the weather was warm.

Pickpockets, I thought.

"Our hostess awaits us," Holmes said.

I saw her then, Lady Carlotta, standing alongside the drive. She was impossible to miss in her bright green silk gown, with a scarf drooping flag-like atop the peak of her tall, cone-shaped green hat.

"Time to speak with Galahad," Holmes said. "Would you please do what you can to set the lady's mind at rest?"

We approached. Lady Carlotta recognized us, giving a glad little cry and hastening forward.

"Mr. Holmes! Dr. Watson! Welcome to Galahad's Castle! What a wonderful occasion! Our turnout is even larger than I had hoped!" Her smile radiated cheerfulness.

We stepped out of the flow on the gravel pathway, but Holmes continued to scan the crowd.

I returned her smile. "A grand day for the Castle."

She touched a hand to her hat, close enough for me to catch the violet scent of her perfume.

"Do I look silly in this big green dunce cap?" she asked.

"Quite the contrary," I said.

"It's Roderick's doing. He wants our anniversary toast to be the highlight of the castle dedication, you see. So, I must dress the part of a medieval lady. At least it makes me look a bit more regal and less of an American commoner."

She paused, and seemed to notice that Holmes was ignoring her. "I'm talking too much, aren't I? I'm all a-twitter, I must say."

"The citizens seem excited as well," I said.

"Decked out for the occasion, like me."

Several women had pinned colorful scarves of red or blue or green to their jackets. Many of the men had doffed their coats in the warm sunlight and moved about in shirtsleeves, a green scarf tied round each man's upper right arm. I could see smoke rising from the coals of several fire pits across the field. Rich smells of roasting meat wafted through the sunlit air. Not far from us, a fat roasting pig turned on a spit, cranked by a large burly man. His green scarf had been tied round his forehead, giving him a piratical air.

"Why the green scarves?" I asked.

"Those are my husband's yeomen," said Lady Carlotta. "Here to assist, however they can. Everyone should have a good time."

We moved closer to the castle, where a square area had been roped off. "That will be for the swordplay," Lady Carlotta said. "Wooden swords, of course. No one should be injured. My husband wants no sorrow here today. We are building something wonderful, and the people know it. The opportunities for employment would sustain many of them throughout the year."

"No wonder they are so enthusiastic," I said.

"And there's my husband now. All in green."

I recognized Galahad at one of the amusement booths, handing out rings to children for the ring-toss.

And beside him stood Holmes, who, unnoticed by us, had slipped away and now appeared to be in urgent conversation with our host.

"What's that about?" asked Lady Carlotta.

"He moves in his own ways," I said. "But I would guess it has to do with the bank loan."

"What?"

"The bank president, that fellow Sherwood, was discussing the project with Holmes yesterday. I didn't catch it all, but it was something about collateral."

"The mineral rights. I know about that."

I shrugged. Holmes and Galahad were now face to face. Galahad appeared to be making up his mind.

Then he turned and led the way into the castle. Holmes followed.

"Where are they going?"

"I have no idea," I said.

One of the yeomen approached us. A burly chap with a flourishing black beard, he glanced back at the castle and then asked, "What's happening, your ladyship?"

"Something to do with the bank loan," she said, flicking her eyes at me.

"That's only my guess," I said hastily, drawing on my prepared explanation. "Mr. Holmes met with the bank president yesterday. I heard the word collateral."

"They always want more collateral," said Lady Carlotta. "My father told me that about bankers."

"We certainly wouldn't want anything to interfere with the project, Dr. Watson," the yeoman said.

He turned to several more green-banded men who had come towards us. "Right lads?"

"It's certainly not up to me," I said.

"Easy enough for you to say—you don't have any stake in the matter," said the yeoman. "If this doesn't go through, we won't have jobs and we'll have to bear the disappointment of our wives and children. But you'll just go blithely back to your rooms on Baker Street."

"I told you, it's not up to me."

"I thought Mr. Holmes was brought in to solve the murders of those two people at the bank," said another.

"The police did, yes."

"So why would the bank president—"

I cut him off. "I don't know, I tell you! I didn't hear their conversation. Just a few words after Mr. Holmes came out from the man's office."

"I think we'd better ask him ourselves," said another yeoman. "Come, lads."

They headed for the castle front entrance, where Galahad and Holmes had gone.

"I'm coming with you," said Lady Carlotta.

"Certainly, my lady," said the first yeoman.

"I do hope Roderick doesn't get upset by this," Lady Carlotta said as we walked towards the castle. "He cares too much, you see. The poor dear. The strain on him has been very great."

We met Holmes and Galahad as they were coming out the front door. Galahad scowled grimly.

"What's wrong, sweetheart?" asked Lady Carlotta.

"Mr. Homes was just leaving," came the curt reply.

"I thought he and Dr. Watson would be at the ceremony?"

"I cannot rely on his loyalty. Loyalty is everything."

"Our disagreement has nothing to do with loyalty," Holmes said.

"Then what has happened?"

"We disagree on the value of my relics," said Galahad. "The banker Sherwood wants them for additional collateral, and Mr. Holmes thinks they're worthless."

"I did not say that. I merely said that a prudent lender would want a competent appraisal."

"An appraisal would be meaningless. My relics have no value other than their ability to inspire the public. And when they are enshrined in my museum and given their proper pride of place, they will be most inspirational indeed. Mr. Holmes, you must make Sherwood understand. My castle restoration must go forward."

"I can do no more than relate the facts as I see them," Holmes said.

Galahad's tone grew distinctly cold. "I had hoped to have you at my side, watching our ceremony."

"Might Watson and I be permitted to watch from the lawn with the other citizens?"

"For all I care, sir, you can watch it from hell!"

He turned and stalked back into the cavernous great hall.

"Come, Watson," Holmes said. "We are not welcome here, and this is, after all, the Earl's private property."

When we were out of earshot, I asked, "How can we guard Lady Carlotta if they banish us from the ceremony?"

Holmes said nothing.

Chapter 31: Violet

When her vision cleared, Violet found she was lying on the floor of the cottage. The heat from the flames all around licked her skin, and smoke still filled the air, although it was marginally thinner down here closer to the ground.

Preston was bending over her, for once shaken out of his usual maddeningly indolent calm. His expression was taut.

"Violet! Wake up! We need to get you out of here."

Violet coughed, trying to blink the sting of smoke out of her eyes. "I'm awake."

Her head was throbbing, but she didn't think she was otherwise hurt—

Her stomach dropped. "I can't move my leg!"

She couldn't quite manage to keep the sharp note of panic out of her tone. Preston moved aside, turning to look. Violet looked, too, and was able to see the wooden ceiling beam that pinned her leg in place just above her right knee.

Violet squeezed her eyes shut, willing away the pure, primitive terror that was trying to claw out of her chest. For all she was used to risking her life whenever a case demanded, she'd never given much time to imagining the least pleasant ways to die. If she had, being trapped in a burning building and scorched alive would have been near to the top of her list, though.

"Hold on," Preston said.

Violet coughed again. It was getting harder and harder to breathe. "I don't think … I have much choice about that."

Preston bent, trying first to lift, then to shove the beam off her leg. But it must have been one of the major supports of the roof. Blackened with age and the size of a medium grown tree trunk, it probably weighed upwards of six hundred pounds or more. Preston succeeded in shifting it a couple of inches, but that was as much as he could do.

"You're not going to be able to help me," Violet gasped. "You should get out—now, while you still can. There must be a way to break down the door or smash through one of the windows."

Preston turned to stare at her. His own eyes were reddened, streaming from the smoke, but his mouth was set in a grim line. "Not a chance. Either we both walk out of here alive or neither of us does."

"What?" It was Violet's turn to stare in shock.

Preston's jaw tightened. "I'm going to pretend you don't sound so surprised right about now."

"That's just stupid." Violet struggled to sit up, then fell back, gasping at the sharp pain that stabbed through her leg. "You shouldn't sacrifice yourself—"

Preston cut her off. "Not arguing." He bent again, grasping hold of the far end of the beam with both hands. His muscles shook with the strain and stood out on his neck like cords. But the beam lifted, slowly but surely, until it was a good six inches off the ground.

Violet yanked her foot and leg out, and Preston let the wood drop to the floor with a crash.

"Think you can walk?" he asked.

Violet tried moving, bending her knee up. "I think so." Her leg hurt, and she'd probably have a bruise the size of a soup tureen in the morning, always assuming that she lived that long. But it didn't feel broken. She'd had enough experience with broken bones to be able to tell the difference.

Preston got to his feet and held out a hand to her, which she ignored, even though her leg was threatening to buckle under her when she tried to put weight on it. "I'm fine."

"Now who's being stupid?" Without waiting for her to answer, he wrapped his fingers around hers and helped her to stand.

Violet stumbled, falling hard against him as she tried to regain her footing. His hands gripped her upper arms, and for a moment they stared at each other, eyes locked. Then Violet jerked away—managing to stand on her own two feet this time—and Preston turned to seize hold of one of the chairs from beside the hearth, which had so far miraculously escaped catching fire.

He swung it in a wide arc, smashing it into the nearest window. The glass shattered. The outside shutters quivered, but then burst open at his second blow.

"Come on!" Preston held out a hand, and this time Violet took it, letting him help her up to the window ledge, where she was able to scramble through and land hard on the ground below. A moment later, Preston followed, landing with a good deal more agility than she had done. But at the moment, Violet couldn't find it in herself to care.

She bent over, her thoughts blank except for the sheer relief of being able to fill her lungs with the comparatively clean outside air.

Out of the corner of her eye, she saw Preston straighten and start towards the surrounding tree line.

"Where are you going?"

He turned his head but didn't stop walking. "Someone sure doesn't want us looking around here. Thought I'd try to find out why." He paused, then added, "You coming?"

Violet stared at him for a moment. Then she nodded, forcing her exhausted muscles to work again. "Of course."

She really had gotten lucky. Her right leg throbbed with every step, but it held her weight as she followed Preston into the trees and along a wooded path that looked as though it had been trampled down by deer.

"Why this way?" she asked. Instinctively, she lowered her voice to a murmur. Despite the growing heat of the day, the cold sweat drying on her skin made her tense against a shiver.

"Because someone's dragged something heavy along this way not too long ago. See?" Preston pointed to the ground.

To Violet, the signs weren't at first glance obvious, but the more she looked, the more she saw: a crushed flower by the side of the path. A broken branch. A patch of dead leaves that had clearly been disturbed.

Preston seemed to read the marks on the ground as easily as newspaper headlines, striding along without hesitation and occasionally choosing to veer off in a new direction.

Although he wasn't entirely relaxed. At some point, he'd drawn his gun and now held it at the ready.

He stopped, scenting the air. "Smell that?" he asked.

"I doubt I'm going to be able to smell anything but smoke for weeks."

"This is more smoke. But older. It's not just the cottage; someone's been lighting fires straight up ahead there." He pointed before continuing to stride ahead until, pushing through a gap in the trees, they came in sight of a charred and blackened hole in the ground.

Debris and what looked like charred bits of paper were scattered all around. But what caught Violet's attention were the pair of men's boots that were partially sticking out of a mound of earth in the center of the fire pit, as though someone had been trying to bury them and had been interrupted halfway through.

No. Her insides tightened as she realized they weren't just boots; they were attached to a pair of legs that had likewise been partially buried and that—presumably—were attached to the rest of the dead body.

Preston had seen it, too. He stiffened and surveyed the small clearing for a moment, gun still at the ready. Then he moved forwards with the same predatory grace as before, crouching down to brush away the layer of covering dirt.

Violet swallowed, then went to help clear the soil from the other side, brushing dirt from where she judged the corpse's torso would be, trying to sift it with her fingers to avoid losing any potential evidence that might have been buried here, too.

Preston looked at her. His face was still smeared with sweat and ash from the fire, sharpening the planes and angles of his cheekbones.

"You sure—"

Violet locked her jaw. "Finish that sentence, and I'll be more than happy to forget that you saved my life back there."

She could feel Preston's gaze on her for another long moment, but he didn't argue.

Violet kept going with the grisly task at hand. The body was definitely that of a man. Her fingers found the buttons on a well-made suit coat and the chain of a watch.

All the same, though, when they had brushed dirt away from the dead man's face, she stumbled to her feet, one hand clamped over her mouth to force down the wave of sickness that had struck her.

Preston tilted his head back. "Know him?" She would have expected censure, possibly mockery, but instead his voice was quiet. Maybe even sympathetic?

Violet swallowed hard again, then nodded, still staring down at the corpse's slack, lifeless face.

She'd seen dead bodies before, far too many of them. But none of them had belonged to the man who'd hired her for the job she was currently on.

Chapter 32: Lucy

"Good masters and sweet ladies!" From where we watched atop the castle tower, Sir Galahad's voice rang out above the noise of the crowd below. "I bid you good morning and welcome you to this fair estate."

He stood at the waist-high stone balustrade that enclosed the circular space, dressed—despite the heat of the day—in a green velvet tunic and cloak that were trimmed with white ermine fur. A gold torque encircled his throat, and a crown rested against his brow.

Merlin, garbed in sober black tunic and hose, was positioned on Sir Galahad's left, although he stood a little further back from the balustrade. He held a tray bearing two bronze chalices that I recognized from the artifact room. As he set the tray down on a low table, I could see that an amber liquid filled both chalices.

To Galahad's right, Lady Carlotta looked ready to wilt—or possibly faint—under the burden of a purple and gold brocade gown and matching headdress. She kept swaying a little and putting a hand out to steady herself against the low stone wall—and every time she did, I could feel my nerves ratchet another notch tighter.

The summer sun was broilingly hot up here, and—more importantly—dazzlingly bright. I kept having to squint in order to keep close watch on Galahad and the others, which was doing nothing to lessen the tension that knotted my spine. Nor was the fact that Jack and I were, of necessity, placed a good fifteen feet away from them.

There were no hiding places on the tower's flat rooftop, which was as barren as a cast-iron griddle. Jack and I, at Holmes's instructions, were positioned just inside the partially opened wooden door that opened from the stairwell onto the roof.

The stairway was windowless, heavily shadowed, and so far, none of the three we were watching had seen us, distracted as they were by the sea of visitors who covered the castle gardens and grounds below.

"Any idea what your father is expecting?" Jack asked in a near-soundless murmur.

The same tension that gripped me was affecting him, too. I could see it in the rigidity of his shoulders, the way his gaze moved continually from Galahad to Merlin to Carlotta and back again.

"Roughly," I whispered back. "He didn't go terribly deeply into specifics."

One side of Jack's mouth tipped up just a fraction. "That's a first."

We both knew that right up until the end of a case, Holmes gave away information with all the willingness of a dragon hoarding gold.

"I know. But I did see him go off with Galahad for a private word earlier. And he told me that you and I are here to, quote, ensure that Galahad obeys instructions."

"And presumably to act as a failsafe in case he doesn't?"

"Presumably."

Outside, Galahad stretched his arms wide, as though to embrace the crowd. "Presently, we will have a jousting match featuring two of my knights, and the fair Lady Carlotta will bestow the queen's badge of favor on the man who most exemplifies the ideals of chivalry."

He put an arm around Carlotta, dragging her forwards to join him at the stone railing. Carlotta looked paler and more likely to faint than ever, but she smiled weakly, clinging to her husband with one hand and using the other to wave a bright green scarf in the air. That must be the badge of favor that she would bestow upon the favorite for the jousting tournament.

Galahad's voice rang out again. "For today, good and loyal subjects, my kingdom is yours, and I invite you to take part in all its delights!"

"So the success of our plan hinges on a man who thinks he's some kind of king following your father's orders," Jack murmured beside me. "What could possibly go wrong there?"

Galahad turned, beckoning Merlin to step forward. "And now, my Lady Carlotta and I would like to propose a toast!" he cried out. He handed one of the chalices to his wife, then gripped the second one and raised it aloft.

Chapter 33: Watson

Ten minutes earlier.

Without explanation, Holmes led me around the massive stone walls of the castle, to the ruined tower.

His gaze was directed upwards, at the broken walls and curving stone steps that loomed above us. I saw the tower top, and the jagged battlements from which Rose, Galahad's first wife, had fallen to her death.

"Bring Lestrade," Holmes said. "And make haste, old friend. We cannot do this alone."

I agreed and left him, making my way through the crowd. Clearly, something was about to happen. But what? My thoughts turned to Lady Carlotta, and the fear her father had expressed. Would Galahad attempt a murder? Surely not, I thought. Not in such public view. That would be utter madness. But how sane was Galahad, really? His emotional outburst over the value of his relics: that was not rational. Nor was his curt dismissal of Holmes.

Around me people had spread blankets on the ground, some with picnic hampers yet unopened. Most were watching the tower, but a few gave me wary glances as I threaded my way alongside their little groups, aiming for the tall iron gates at the front entrance to the castle grounds.

I felt a hand tap my shoulder. "Dr. Watson!" It was Preston, the Pinkerton's agent, accompanied by a tall, dark-haired woman whom I didn't recognize. "Where's Mr. Holmes?"

"At the castle." I pointed towards the tower, visible above the castle walls. "But he has urgent business at hand just now. Can the matter wait?"

Preston's answer was typically laconic. "Only if you think the discovery of a murder victim is something that can be put off to a more convenient time."

I stared. "You have discovered a body? Whose? And where?"

"At a cottage on the estate grounds. Lestrade has taken charge. As for whose body it is"—Preston and the dark-haired woman exchanged a look—"well, that's something I'd rather take up with Mr. Holmes."

A short while later, we were back at the tower.

Trumpets blared. The buzz of the crowd diminished. The trumpets blared again, and then a voice from above rang out.

"For today, good and loyal subjects, my kingdom is yours, and I invite you to take part in all its delights!"

Looking up, I saw Sir Galahad standing at the tower parapet to address the crowd.

At last I caught sight of Holmes's tall figure amongst the waiting spectators, and shouldered my way towards him, with Preston and his companion following.

Holmes's sharp gaze took in the expression on the Pinkerton agent's face. "Something has happened."

"We found a body." It was the dark-haired woman who answered. "A man's body, buried in a shallow grave not far from here."

"Ah." Holmes's gaze narrowed briefly as he studied the woman's face. Then he said, "I take it you recognized—"

His words were drowned out as Sir Galahad's voice rang out from above us again. "And now, my Lady Carlotta and I would like to propose a toast!" he cried. "To King Arthur! To our fair England! And to all the visitors whom we are honored to welcome to our kingdom today!"

He handed one chalice to Lady Carlotta, then raised the other golden vessel to his lips.

He drank.

Holmes moved with the lightning speed of which only he was capable, racing for the castle entrance and tossing the words at us back over his shoulder.

"Come with me at once! We have but one chance to prevent another death!"

I ran after him, my mind in a whirl as the evidence and the hints Holmes had given assembled in my mind.

Lady Carlotta would drink from the chalice, the drug would take effect and it would induce hallucinations. Fearful and disturbed, she would rush about on the tower in an agitated condition. She would come too close to the edge. Then, with no witnesses save Galahad and his faithful cohort Merlin, she would be induced to fall, or perhaps her own movements would be sufficient to cause disaster. Whether pushed or not, she would plummet to a horrible end, just as Lady Rose had done.

Unless we could get there first.

CHAPTER 34: LUCY

"Ladies and gentlemen," Galahad began again. Then he stopped, coughing.

He doubled over, stepping back from the parapet and pressing a hand to his mouth as he gasped for air. I froze.

Beside him, Merlin turned to Galahad with alarm. "My Lord? Are you ill?"

Galahad swayed and would have fallen if Merlin had not caught him under the arms and lowered him gently to the flagstones.

Jack gave me a questioning look. I dug my nails into my palms and silently shook my head. If we acted too early, we would lose the chance of collecting eyewitness evidence that would prove our murderer's guilt.

Wide-eyed, Lady Carlotta crouched down beside her husband, who was writhing on the ground as though in terrible pain.

"Galahad?" She took hold of his shoulder. "Galahad!"

Sir Galahad moaned, but didn't open his eyes. Carlotta and Merlin looked at one another across his prostrate body.

Then Merlin seized hold of Sir Galahad's arms and started to drag him across the tower, towards the side facing away from the crowd.

"Are you sure this will work?" he panted.

"It has to!" Carlotta quickened her steps to keep up with him, towing Galahad's feet. Her voice was quicker, sharper than I'd yet heard from her, her movements decisive. "Everyone knows he's completely unbalanced with all of his Camelot nonsense. The verdict will be that he had a sudden fit of madness and threw himself off of the tower. We're both here to witness it. If we tell the same story, no one can prove us wrong. If you like, we can tell the police that he was babbling about Rose—imply that he was overcome with guilt over her death. That way, all your efforts to suggest that he killed her won't go to waste."

Sir Galahad suddenly stopped writhing, tore himself free of their grasp, and stood up.

"I am sorry to put a crimp in your plans. But Mr. Holmes warned me in advance against drinking the ceremonial toast, so I had one of my knights substitute a fresh pitcher for the one you had prepared."

Lady Carlotta and Merlin stared at him, their faces fixed in identical looks of consternation.

Merlin took a menacing half-step towards Galahad, but before he could enact whatever violence he intended, Jack had stepped out from the stairwell. Taking hold of Merlin's arm, Jack twisted it up and behind Merlin's back so quickly that the other man had no time to react.

"Let him go!" Lady Carlotta's voice rose to a shrill scream. "He was only trying to defend himself!"

She was inching her way forwards, towards Jack and Merlin.

I stepped out from concealment as well, leveling my Ladysmith revolver at her.

"I really wouldn't try it. You have at best about five minutes until more Scotland Yard officers arrive to take you and your confederate into custody. If I were you, I'd devote them to coming up with a more convincing line of defense."

Lady Carlotta stared at me. Her face, too, seemed to have sharpened, her features no longer insipidly pretty but twisted with the fury of a rat caught in a trap.

"I—I—My husband is quite mad—he tried to attack us both!"

"A worthy effort, Lady Carlotta," Holmes said from the doorway. He stepped out onto the roof. "However, you may feel less inclined to defend Mr. Calloway there once I tell you that your father's dead body was discovered just outside Calloway's cottage less than a quarter of an hour ago."

Lady Carlotta jerked backwards in shock, all the color draining from her face. "I—I don't believe you."

Holmes shrugged. "That, of course, is your prerogative. But you can see for yourself in a few minutes' time. Your testimony will be needed for a positive identification."

Holmes's calm indifference seemed to convince Lady Carlotta. She stared at Holmes for another moment. Then she rounded on Calloway in a whirl of velvet skirts.

"You killed my father!"

"Shut up!" Calloway's face twisted in fury. "Do you want to get us both hanged? Don't say another word!"

"I don't care!" Lady Carlotta's voice broke into heaving sobs as she flung herself on Calloway, trying to claw at his face. "I don't care!"

Holmes caught hold of her from one side. Watson, who had caught up to Holmes and come out onto the roof to join us, took hold of Carlotta's other arm, and together they dragged her off and away from Calloway.

Sir Galahad watched them, his expression sorrowful. Sorrowful, I thought, but not entirely shocked.

He'd lived with Lady Carlotta, had closer contact with her

than any of us—enough that the discovery of her real motivations hadn't come as a much of a surprise, at least not to him.

Maybe in the end, Sir Galahad had a stronger grip on reality than any of us had given him credit for.

"You should address your audience," Holmes told him. "Give them some reassurance that all is well."

Sir Galahad swallowed, nodded, then cleared his throat and stepped back to the battlements. "Beg pardon, ladies and gentlemen! Brevity being the soul of wit, we are bringing the speeches of this ceremony to a thundering halt. I take it no one objects? Splendid. Enjoy the day, everyone!"

CHAPTER 35: WATSON

Lestrade said, "I'll begin with the attempted murder of Sir Galahad."

We were all seated around the large round table within the barren expanse of Galahad's great hall: Lestrade, Holmes, me, Lucy, Jack, Galahad, and the two Pinkerton operatives. Lady Carlotta and Calloway, in handcuffs, occupied the last two chairs. Two local constables stood behind them.

Calloway said, "I have nothing to say."

"I don't have to listen to this," said Lady Carlotta. "Take me somewhere else."

"You will need to answer questions," Lestrade said.

"Why? You have nothing but words against me—from eavesdropping on my conversation with Calloway."

"You were seen dragging your husband—"

"Who was shamming incapacity. But he is alive and unharmed."

"Because you were stopped—"

She interrupted. "Look, inspector whatever-your-name-is. If you want to arrest me, then go on and do that. I doubt my husband will even press charges."

She glanced expectantly in her husband's direction, but Sir Galahad said nothing. He was staring at the floor with an unreadable expression on his face, and didn't even glance in his wife's direction.

Lady Carlotta looked momentarily taken aback, but rallied and went on. "And I doubt you will get a conviction if he does. As long as Mr. Calloway here isn't saying anything."

"Do you still maintain that he killed your father?"

I thought Lady Carlotta's face blanched slightly, but she had evidently decided that a policy of flat denial was her best option. With only a slight hitch in her voice, she said, "I—I shall reserve judgement on that."

Lestrade appeared perplexed.

"There are two other murders for which you will be required to answer, Lady Carlotta," said Sherlock Holmes. "Mr. Huxley and Mrs. Clair."

"Huxley was alive and well when I said goodbye to him at the bank. And my father and I went straight home from there. The servants saw me arrive, with my father, before our evening supper was served. And they saw us at the dinner table and at bed time."

"You arrived at Trent Hall in a cab," Holmes said.

"So?"

"I wonder why you would take a cab. It is barely a two-minute walk to Trent Hall."

"My father is old. Was."

"Yet the next morning he told me he walked for hours. To clear his mind."

Lady Carlotta shrugged.

"Huxley put the two of you into the cab, did he not?"

"If you say so."

"The bank doorman says so. He generally hails cabs for departing visitors. On this occasion, he recalls you linking your arm in Huxley's and striding across the walkway and stopping. Then you said something to Huxley and he hailed the cab."

"That is not a crime."

"But it did make an impression and provide an impartial witness to your departure."

"What of it?"

"To understand, we need to go back to the sequence of events here in Tottenham that resulted in the death of Mr. Huxley." Holmes looked at Lestrade. "With your permission, Inspector?"

Lestrade nodded.

"Very well. You initiated the sequence, Mr. Preston, when you traced one of the stolen bearer bond coupons to the Tottenham Bank and met with Mr. Sherwood, the bank president."

"He refused to cooperate," Preston said.

"But he thought it prudent to notify you, Sir Galahad, of the Pinkerton inquiry, the funds from the coupon had been deposited into your account."

"What?" Galahad seemed bewildered. "I never spoke to him."

"Quite right," said Holmes. "For such a detail, Sherwood thought it would suffice to notify Calloway, your man of business. When you heard the news, Calloway, you told Lady Carlotta, she told her father, and Huxley's fate was sealed."

"We did suspect Brown of the initial bond robbery," said Preston.

"So Huxley could not be allowed to continue in the knowledge that there were additional bonds in the safety deposit box, namely the bonds that Brown had stolen. Your safety deposit box was the perfect hiding place. When the legitimate dowry bonds had been vetted by your solicitors before your wedding, it was an easy matter for Brown to slip the stolen bonds into the packet for safe storage."

"I had no idea," said Galahad.

"Things went smoothly for a time, until the dowry bonds had all been cashed. Then it came time to replenish your overdrawn cash account, and Mr. Huxley followed his routine practice and did what he had always done. He clipped another coupon and cashed it. However, he failed to note that the bond coupon was not one that had come with the dowry."

Lady Carlotta sat rigid and silent.

"Then you heard from Sherwood, who would have said that the US Government and Her Majesty's Government were concerned in the matter." He glanced at Preston. "You said something to that effect, Mr. Preston?"

"I did lay it on a bit thick, I suppose," Preston said.

"So, Lady Carlotta, you believed that at some point governmental channels would lead to an official inspection of your husband's safety deposit box, so the bonds were no longer safe. You had to get them out. You and your father met with Huxley. You taxed him with his incompetence, namely that he had cashed in a bond that was your personal property, not property of your husband. You brought your key, and demanded to see the bonds. You and your father went with him to the vault and emptied the deposit box. Then you said your very public farewell to Huxley. You stepped into the cab, but you did not drive home to Trent Hall. Instead, you drove to the back of the bank, and you left the cab. The cabman will remember."

"Try proving that," Lady Carlotta said.

"Ah, well, the cabman may be reluctant to admit it, but he does remember, nonetheless." Holmes gave another of his tight little smiles. "The cabman was Mr. Calloway."

"Fiddlesticks."

"The bank doorman would have noticed that Calloway was

not one of the regular cabman, so to hail the cab, you used the doomed Mr. Huxley."

Calloway showed his teeth in a confident smile. "As Lady Carlotta said, prove it."

Holmes looked at him without expression. "To begin, there is this photograph, found in your cottage." He held up the photograph of the two children which Flynn and Becky had found. "It ought to be easy enough to identify the subjects as yourself and Lady Carlotta. Children may change as they grow older, but fundamental bone structure does not. Any expert will, I'm sure, be quite confident in making an identification. And regardless, inquiries in the States will, I am confident, reveal that you and Lady Carlotta have been acquainted with one another from childhood. You have been planning this crime for quite some time—years, in fact. You inveigled yourself into a position as Sir Galahad's right-hand man, then orchestrated the death of the first Lady Trent in the same way you sought to bring about Sir Galahad's: by giving her various herbal concoctions that resulted in a highly impressionable, destabilized mental state. You dosed her with one of your brews, then while she was still under the influence, told her to meet you at the top of the castle tower.

"Dazed and stupefied by the drugs she had been given, she obeyed. If she had not conveniently fallen to her death that day, I have no doubt that you would have tried again. But your plan succeeded. Lady Rose Trent died at a time when you yourself had an unimpeachable alibi. Of course, Sir Galahad also had an alibi. But that suited your purposes well enough, for at the time, you had no wish for him to be charged with the murder. That was to come later.

"Following Lady Rose's death, you arranged for Sir Galahad to be introduced to your childhood friend, Carlotta Brown." Holmes nodded to Lady Carlotta. "And again, matters worked out in perfect accordance with your plans. Sir Galahad, if not in love with Lady Carlotta, was at least captivated enough to propose marriage. A prospect made more appealing, I'm sure, by the dowry which Lady Carlotta's father promised."

Sir Galahad winced visibly. Lady Carlotta continued to look stony-faced.

"Carlotta and Sir Galahad were married, and the two of you, working together, began your campaign to lay the groundwork for a mental breakdown that would ultimately result in Galahad's death."

Sir Galahad's jaw tightened, but he still did not look up.

"You also hoped to plant suspicion that Lady Rose Trent had died by murder, and that Sir Galahad was responsible. To that end, Lady Carlotta, your father approached me with a story that Sir Galahad was a wife-killer, and that he feared for your life. Additionally, you, Mr. Calloway, broke into Dr. Norton's office at a time of day when the theft could not fail to be noticed, and purloined the doctor's files on Lady Rose. The purpose was not to obtain the files themselves, for they would have told us nothing beyond that which Dr. Norton was able to recount. No, your aim in stealing them was to cast further suspicion on Sir Galahad—to suggest that he was the thief. You wished to create the illusion that he was aware of some detail in the files which would point to his guilt, and thus had tried to suppress them by bold-faced robbery and assault on the doctor. In fleeing the doctor's office, you were nearly caught by Sergeant Kelly here, who may be able to identify you on that account."

Jack shifted position, studying Calloway. "I can't swear to a positive identification. But I could certainly testify that the man who robbed Dr. Norton was Mr. Calloway's height and build."

Mr. Calloway looked momentarily triumphant, until Holmes went on, "In any case, the cab company manager will be able to identify you. You rented the cab that carried Lady Carlotta and her father to and from Mr. Huxley's offices."

Calloway remained silent.

"Then, Lady Carlotta, you and your father entered the bank through the rear entrance. You walked quickly to Huxley's office and hid yourselves behind the curtain, one on either side of the window. You, Carlotta, waited till Huxley sat at his desk. You distracted him while your father stabbed him with the dagger you brought from the castle. The dagger, you thought, taken with the message 'for my sins,' would implicate your husband's vigilante knights. You did the murder, cleared off Huxley's desk, and wrote the message. You had already prepared the ground by spreading rumours through Mrs. Clair, Mr. Huxley's assistant, of his supposedly improper behavior towards you. Calloway waited below the window while you dropped Huxley's files and documents down to him. He carried the documents the short distance to the cab. You and your father then left the bank, now closed for the evening, by the same rear doorway through which you had entered. You then drove the short distance to Trent Hall and made that show of arriving which your servants remember."

"Lies," said Lady Carlotta.

Holmes went on as if she had not spoken. "Brown still had the bonds on his person. But he had one more task to perform. He had to come to London to meet with me, to establish his alibi for the cruelest step of all, the murder of Mrs. Clair. That was done because she might have revealed that you, Lady Carlotta, were the source—the sole source, I might add—of the rumours about Mr. Huxley's unchivalrous behavior. That crime, Mr. Calloway, you performed the next day, duplicating the message and method that Lady Carlotta and her father had used for Mr. Huxley. Then you took the loan application materials to your cottage and burned them. Brown returned. You met him at your cottage and killed him. You took the bonds and the safe deposit box key from his pockets. You had no use for the safe deposit key, since the box was empty, so you dropped the key into the ashes of Huxley's papers. You were interrupted in the burial of Mr. Brown by two children, who were in my employ. You imprisoned them, thinking you would deal with them later, after you had put in an appearance at the Tottenham Bank. You hurried over to the office of the bank president, where you gave an affecting show of concern for Galahad's loan application."

"I was trying to help Galahad."

"That is a lie. You and Lady Carlotta planned to kill him." Holmes shrugged. "In any event, the key you discarded was later recovered by one of the children you temporarily imprisoned, and it proved very useful in unravelling the mystery."

We all sat silent.

Calloway turned his eyes to Carlotta, a long, searching look. For a moment, I wondered. Had he done the murders for her, hoping that the two of them could make a life together?

"I won't talk, darling," he said. "Don't worry."

Carlotta averted her gaze.

"So about the bonds," said Calloway. "Now is the time to talk turkey. How badly do you want the bonds back? What is my conviction worth to you?"

Lestrade said, "You will tell us where the bonds are, and perhaps we may request mercy in your sentence."

"Spare me from the hangman, you mean? I don't think so. Not for two million."

Holmes said, "I should not advocate negotiating with this criminal. I suggest we postpone that inquiry for the moment."

He gave a long glance at Violet, but said nothing more, and Lestrade, after a moment's pause, stepped forward.

"Lady Carlotta Trent, Peter Calloway, I'm placing you under arrest for the murders of Mr. Huxley, Mr. Brown, and Mrs. Clair. You do not have to say anything, but anything you do say will be taken down and may be given in evidence."

He gestured to the two waiting constables, who hauled the handcuffed prisoners to their feet and marched them towards the door.

Carlotta turned at the last moment to her husband. "Are you really going to allow this, Galahad? Think of the scandal! The smirch on the honour of your family name."

Finally, at that, Sir Galahad's head lifted, and he looked at his wife directly. His lips were compressed as though with pain, but his voice was steady. "The only dishonour I can think of would be to allow you to get away with your crimes."

Epilogue: Violet

Violet made her escape shortly after Lestrade had gone out with his prisoners in tow. Some more of Lestrade's men had arrived and were circling the room, taking written statements from everyone. Violet gave hers as briefly as possible and slipped out.

She ought to have felt triumphant, or at least glad that both murderers had been captured and would be brought to trial. But seeing criminals led away in handcuffs always left her with a hollow, vaguely depressed feeling.

Too many memories.

She had hoped simply to slip out without further conversation, but Mr. Holmes caught up with her just as she was stepping through the castle's arched front entrance.

"Agent Leverton."

Violet turned, suppressing a start of surprise at the use of her last name. "You recognized me, then?"

Mr. Holmes' keen gray eyes held a slight hint of amusement, but oddly, Violet found that she didn't mind. The humor was equally directed at himself as at her.

"A few years may have passed, but I hope I am not yet so aged or infirm that I could fail to recognize a detective who was instrumental in bringing a mutual case to a satisfactory conclusion. You are Leverton, whose work on the Red Circle problem proved quite valuable."

Violet sighed. Then grimaced. Mr. Holmes hadn't asked for any sort of explanation, but she found that she wanted to offer one all the same.

"Mr. Pinkerton—Mr. Allan Pinkerton, the founder of Pinkerton's Detective Agency—was fairly accepting of female agents. Encouraging, even. He had an entire department filled with 'Pinks' as he called his female operatives. He saw that we could go places where no man could go without suspicion, and that we could get information in ways that would be far more difficult for a man. But then Mr. Pinkerton died, and his sons took over the agency. They've proved … different altogether from their father. Especially in regard to their attitude towards women. For several years, I was tolerated as an agent, having worked for Pinkerton's since the elder Mr. Pinkerton's time. But only just. Generally speaking, the Mr. Pinkertons junior would prefer that women stayed meekly at home, washing their husband's clothes and looking pretty. And they're quite happy to lend aid to any anti-suffragist movements—those trying to prevent women from winning the right to vote. So I—" Violet stopped.

"Impersonate a male agent on occasion?" Mr. Holmes asked.

Violet raised her head. "Only when it's more advantageous to do so! I'm not ashamed of being female, far from it. Nor do I believe that women are in any way less capable than men. But the world in general is more in alignment with the second generation of Pinkerton's than the first in their attitudes towards the female sex. And sometimes it's simply more convenient to play the part of a man."

Mr. Holmes raised an eyebrow, the gleam of humor in his eyes once more apparent. "Particularly when you are forced to contact a stuffy, hidebound English—male—detective—and are unsure of whether or not you will be taken seriously as a female?"

Violet found herself smiling. "In fairness, I was just as concerned with my reception at Scotland Yard as I was with you on the Red Circle case. But yes."

Mr. Holmes said nothing, but once again Violet felt compelled to go on. If for no other reason than that she was certain that Sherlock Holmes, like Preston, would make a far better ally than adversary.

"I'm no longer with Pinkerton's." She didn't feel compelled to explain the ins and outs of that, however, so she went on without pause. "But I was hired as an independent inquiry agent by Mr. Brown."

"Indeed." Mr. Holmes' tone was one of having just received confirmation of a fact that he'd already known quite well.

"How did you—" Violet began. "Never mind. Of course, you probably deduced as much. Mr. Brown and some business associates of his were the driving force behind the stolen bonds scheme. But then Mr. Brown was double-crossed by his partners. He'd taken a million dollars worth of the stolen bonds and camouflaged them with legitimate bonds. As you said earlier, that was when he put up his daughter's dowry and got her married to an English nobleman of questionable sanity."

"One whose estate sits upon a veritable gold-mine of mineral rights," Holmes added. "Which Brown planned to exploit to the fullest extent possible once Galahad was out of the way and his daughter had inherited the castle and the lands it sits on."

"Yes. But there were three million dollars worth of bonds stolen, and Brown only had the one million. The rest of the bonds had gone missing—purloined by Brown's partners. So he hired me to come over here and get them back."

"I see."

Mr. Holmes's gaze held no judgment, but Violet felt her cheeks flush. "I wasn't actually going to do as he asked! If it's dratted hard to work for Pinkerton's as a female agent these days, it's even harder to find people willing to hire a lone female detective. But I still have some moral and professional standards! I was willing to take Brown's job—and his money to pay my way over here—but I knew quite well that he was a crook. My plan was to find the bonds, return them to the US Treasury Department, and see Brown and his business partners thrown in jail for the theft."

"An admirable aim. And not that my opinion is of great relevance, but I believe you," Mr. Holmes added.

"Thank you." Violet was surprised by the relief she felt at that. "I've a lead—a strong suspicion of where I think the bonds might be. But I'd prefer to follow it up on my own."

"I see. Without, for example, Mr. Preston's involvement?"

"To quote something he'd probably say, I'd rather chew on a box of rusty nails." Violet felt slightly guilty as she said it. He'd saved her life just that morning, after all. But then she doubted Preston would be any more willing to share the credit for recovering the bonds with her than she was with him. They were both just born and bred that way.

Mr. Holmes studied her a moment from under half-lidded eyes, then seemed to come to a decision. "Very well. I can offer to delay Mr. Preston's departure from here for perhaps a quarter of an hour. When I left the room, he was still giving a statement to one of Lestrade's men as to the events of this morning. But being a man of intelligence—and probably having surmised, as I have, that you are the most likely to recover the stolen bonds—I imagine that he will be leaving and eager to pick up your trail quite soon."

Violet nodded. "Thanks for the warning. I'll just have to be sure not to leave a trail for him to follow, then."

* * *

In the end, though, it wasn't Preston who managed to track her down.

Violet had returned to London—had even changed her appearance three times—before the familiar tingling sensation at the back of her neck alerted her to the fact that she was being watched from behind.

She was just crossing Trafalgar Square. It would be evening soon. The famous monument of Nelson atop his towering column cast a long, slanting shadow in the setting sun. Carriages rattled to and fro, the fountains splashed, and the four immense guarding lion statues looked sleepy in the summer heat, despite the crowds of people pressing this way and that.

At least the square was crowded, like most places in central London. Plenty of opportunities to lose herself in the swarm of other pedestrians. Violet quickened her pace, turned onto St. Martin's Lane, and then ducked behind a convenient newspaper stand.

The proprietor of the stand was busy selling papers and tobacco and cigarettes to the businessmen on their way home from offices at this hour of the day. No one gave Violet a second glance.

She waited, watching the passers-by, until a pair of familiar figures came into view.

Violet stepped out from the news stand and moved up behind them.

"I assume that you're looking for me?"

The boy and girl who worked for Mr. Holmes turned, their expressions set in nearly identical looks of chagrin.

"Did Mr. Holmes send you?" Violet asked. She was disappointed at their appearance. She had thought that Mr. Holmes respected her enough to let her carry this final task out in her own way, even if she had to admit that in his place, she might well have sent someone to shadow her.

But the girl shook her head, setting her blond braids swinging. "No. He has no idea that we're here. Flynn followed Mr. Preston from Baker Street last night. Mr. Holmes didn't know about that, either. He thought we were both in the kitchen with Mrs. Hudson. But Flynn saw him meeting with you in the park."

Violet stared, the memory unwinding in her head.

She hadn't recognized him, or even realized that she was being followed after bidding goodbye to Preston that night. Possibly because of the elevation in blood pressure that any encounter with Preston caused, but still. She should have been more alert.

"You were the beggar boy on crutches."

The boy gave her a quick flash of a grin. "That was me."

"Then he followed you to your hotel," the girl went on. "So that we'd know where you were staying. We stayed behind from going to the castle this morning because we wanted to keep a watch on the train station. To see where you went when you came back."

In other words, she'd been thoroughly outsmarted by a couple of children. Violet struggled with it for a moment, but in the end her mouth twitched. "What are your names?"

"I'm Becky. That's Flynn." Becky tipped her head at her companion.

"Well, then, Becky and Flynn. I'm on my way to perform a possibly dangerous errand, and I would prefer not to put either of you at risk. On the other hand, you've certainly both proved that you're more than capable of detective work, and it wouldn't be an entirely bad thing to have a pair of witnesses who know where I am."

Just in case, a voice in the back of her head whispered.

"I propose that you continue to follow me, but from a safe distance—say, about a block. That ought to be easy enough, since I promise not to try to lose you. Don't get any closer, don't approach me directly, and whatever you do, don't come into the building where I'm going." She looked from one of them to the other. "Agreed?"

Flynn and Becky exchanged a glance, then nodded. "Agreed."

Violet started walking again, going about half a block before she allowed herself to look backwards to see whether the children were obeying the terms of their arrangement. They were. Both stood by the newspaper stand, watching, waiting for her to reach the agreed-upon block of distance between them.

A black carriage drawn by a team of four black horses rattled past them, going at least twice as fast as any of the other vehicles in the road. The carriage didn't slow down as it barreled towards her. Despite the summer heat, the driver was dressed in a black cloak, hat, and a heavy black muffler that concealed the lower half of his face.

Warning bells started to sound in Violet's mind. But not quite soon enough.

She'd barely started to step back before the carriage had drawn abreast of her. The door swung open, strong hands seized hold of her, and a pad of something sickly sweet and sticky was pressed against her nose and mouth.

Violet's last sight was of Becky's shocked face and Flynn's wide eyes as both started to run towards her. But darkness was closing in, and her muscles had turned into wet cotton, stopping her from even attempting to fight back as she was hauled inside the black carriage. She heard a shout from the driver, then felt the lurch as the carriage resumed its careening pace down the street.

Then blackness closed in fully, and she knew nothing more.

THE END

Historical Note

This is a work of fiction, and the authors make no claim that any of the historical locations or historical figures appearing in this story had even the remotest connection with the events recounted herein.

However …

1. We drew inspiration for *Galahad's Castle* from two castles in England that are still attracting visitors today. The first is Herstmonceau, located on a 300-acre estate in East Sussex. Built in 1441, the castle lay in ruins until restored in the early twentieth century. It is now the site of many tours and weddings, frequent historical re-enactments, and an annual medieval fair.

2. Our second source of inspiration was Bruce Castle, a 16th century manor house located closer to London, in Tottenham. It is now a museum, open to the public. The castle bears a legend, however, which we found intriguing: in November 1680, Lady Constantina Lucy flung herself from the castle parapet, her child in her arms, and both of them were killed. Her ghost has been seen haunting the castle. According to an 1858 newspaper account, the ghost's "wild form can be seen as she stood on the

fatal parapet, and her despairing cry is heard floating away on the autumnal blast."

3. The Pinkerton's National Detective Agency, founded in 1850, employed a number of female agents. One of the most famous, Kate Warne, frequently used disguises to conceal her activities, which included working for the United States Government and, on one mission, protecting the life of then-president-elect Abraham Lincoln. The division of Pinkerton's that she headed later became the American Secret Service.

Lucy James and Violet Leverton will return.

A Note of Thanks

Thank you for reading *Galahad's Castle*. We hope you've enjoyed it.

As you probably know, reviews make a big difference! So, we also hope you'll consider going back to the Amazon page where you bought the story and uploading a quick review. You can get to that page by going to this link on our website and scrolling down:

sherlockandlucy.com/project/galahad

You can also sign up for our mailing list to receive updates on new stories, special discounts, and 'free days' for some of our other books: www.SherlockandLucy.com

Wondering what happens next?

THE SHERLOCK HOLMES/ LUCY JAMES MYSTERIES

THE LOCH NESS HORROR

BY ANNA ELLIOTT AND CHARLES VELEY

Read the next exciting installment in the Sherlock Holmes and Lucy James series!

A shadowy ruin. A monstrous plot. And unless Sherlock and Lucy can stop an evil mastermind, thousands of innocent lives will end in horror. A fast-paced and thrilling take on a classic Sherlock who-done-it, with unexpected twists and turns, two strong, feisty heroines, and a touch of romance. The Loch Ness Horror stays faithful to the of the beloved original series, while introducing more intriguing relationship dynamics.

Read on for a thrilling preview of

THE **SHERLOCK HOLMES/ LUCY JAMES** MYSTERIES

THE LOCH NESS HORROR

Prologue: Violet

"Still poking that long nose where it doesn't belong, aren't ye, Leverton?"

The man's voice penetrated the fog of Violet's unconsciousness. Smirking, insinuating, and somehow ... familiar?

The words carried her back through the years. Jagged shards of memory stabbed her.

Schoolyard taunts from the other children. *Haggy. Little witch.*

Her father, lying dead on the floor of yet another saloon after Violet had failed—again—to persuade him to come home.

Her mother, white-faced with terror, hissing at her to run, to fetch the police, while the front door of their apartment shuddered under the force of Cassidy's blows.

'Brick' Cassidy—the man who had killed her father in a barroom brawl and then run away—was a drunk with a nasty temper and a subnormal intelligence. But even he was smart enough to realize that he couldn't be prosecuted if the witnesses to his crime were dead.

Violet had tried. She'd run, sick with fear, to the nearest police station and half begged, half dragged the officer on duty to come. But she'd been too late.

After, she'd watched the man who'd killed both her father and her mother being led away in handcuffs, cursing and swearing he'd get even with her when he got out of prison ...

No. Violet slammed the door on those memories. *No.*

Whatever fresh nightmare was in store for her now, she'd at least left that life behind.

The cloying, sickly-sweet smell of chloroform clogged her nose and throat, and whatever surface she lay on rattled and bounced, tossing her painfully from side to side.

A carriage.

It was only a small piece of certainty, but she clung to it all the same. She was in a carriage. Lying on the floor of a carriage with at least one man who thought she was more deeply unconscious than she really was.

Her muscles were refusing to obey her, and she couldn't even force her eyes to open, so it was hard to see how she could turn her wakefulness to any advantage. But maybe if she could straighten her tangled thoughts, think clearly …

Memories returned, no longer knife sharp, but hazy, like stray wisps of cloud.

Walking along a busy London street. A huge black carriage, driven too fast, bearing down on her.

Hands seizing her, a pad pressed over her nose and mouth.

Even in the foggy haze that currently shrouded her, Violet's heart pounded in remembered panic.

This wasn't helping. She took a breath and tried to think.

Another memory-wisp floated across her mind's eye: an image of a boy and a girl, both with blond hair.

The children who worked for Mr. Holmes.

Becky and Flynn.

Yes, that was right. She'd been on her way … on her way *somewhere*, with something pressing, something terribly important to do.

The exact mission she'd been on slipped and slithered away from her when she tried to grasp at it. But the pulse-racing sense of urgency remained.

She'd spotted the children, who had been shadowing her.

She'd told them that they could keep following her at a distance. Which meant that unless Becky and Flynn had been captured, too, there were at least two people in the world who knew what had happened to her.

The man's voice spoke again, and this time it was accompanied by a hard jab in Violet's ribs. He'd prodded her with the toe of his boot.

"Still pryin' into matters that are no concern of yours."

The voice was rough with a thick Scottish brogue. She *knew* whoever was speaking to her. If only she could claw her way back to consciousness—

Urquhart.

The name—just the name—surfaced from the depths of Violet's memory first.

Then a man's face: sallow, sharp-featured, lean, with a sneering smile and hollow cheekbones.

Violet had to clench her teeth to keep from gasping. This time it wasn't a stray wisp of memory that returned, but a solid chunk that hit her like another kick in the ribs.

Owen Urquhart, chemist and right-hand man to Benjamin Blinder, who had stolen one million dollars in bearer bonds from the United States government.

Violet had been trying to get the bonds back. She'd known—or thought she'd known—where they were to be found.

But she hadn't told Sherlock Holmes or anyone else, hadn't wanted to involve anyone else in her mission.

Hadn't wanted to share the credit for the find, a voice at the back of her mind sneered.

Well, what if she hadn't? Recovering the bonds could have gotten her job back. She'd have been an agent of Pinkerton's Detective Agency again, instead of being forced to take whatever freelance work—mostly sordid divorce cases—she could find.

But she'd gone racing off on her own, without any backup except for the two children.

Another familiar voice spoke in her ear. Although it was only one more fragment of memory, this one was particularly sharp-edged.

Preston, looking at her from under half-lidded eyes, and drawling, *Try not to be stupid, Leverton. You just might live longer.*

Even with her face smashed against the floor of the carriage and the accumulated road grit scraping her cheek with every bump, Violet gritted her teeth so hard that her jaw ached. She had to survive this. Wherever Urquhart was taking her, whatever tortures he had planned, she was going to live through them, find a way to escape—and what was more, see Urquhart and Blinder both locked up behind bars.

Because she was *not* going to allow her last act here on earth to be so stupid that it presented Preston with a magnificent opportunity to say, *I told you so.*

Chapter 1: Watson

London, July 1900

I did not know it at the time, but the case of the Loch Ness Horror had already begun, even as Holmes and I were traveling home from Galahad's Castle.

Holmes was in one of his ill-tempered moods. He barely spoke as we rode the train back to London. The day was a hot one, the air inside our cab from Victoria Station felt stifling, and the traffic moved slowly. It took us nearly a half hour to reach Whitehall, normally a five-minute journey.

Then our cab stopped.

"At this rate we won't reach Baker Street for another hour," I said.

Holmes said nothing.

I lifted my window and leaned out to survey the melee of horse-drawn carts and omnibuses and lorries and cabs. The air was filled with the loud and irate protests of drivers and passengers.

"For a Sunday, the streets are unusually crowded," I said.

Holmes said nothing.

"But only in our direction. Traffic coming our way on the other side is flowing freely. I don't see the cause of the delay."

I closed the window, which at least blocked the dust and shut out some of the noise.

Holmes said nothing.

I tried again to engage him in conversation, this time taking a more direct approach.

"Why so glum?" I asked.

"I am preoccupied, Watson," he said.

"Why?"

"Because we failed."

I knew he was referring to the Galahad's Castle case.

"A bit harsh, surely," I replied.

"The term is accurate." He folded his arms across his chest.

"I cannot agree, Holmes," I said. "Two murderers are now imprisoned in Tottenham, thanks to you. That is a success, and a significant one at that."

He shook his head. "I delayed, when I ought to have acted."

"When?"

"This morning I allowed Miss Leverton to pursue a plan she had devised. Out of respect and deference to her abilities, I did not even ask her what her plan was. I simply said I would wait for her to act. I ought to have demanded that she work with me."

"Why?"

"I had deduced what she would do. And if I could do that, others could do so as well, and get there first."

"Get where?"

"To the stolen bonds we had first set out to recover. As you will recall, they are worth one million dollars. Mr. Brown's criminal colleagues have been searching for them ever since Mr. Brown brought them to England. If they have been following him, or following Miss Leverton, it is all too likely that they will have hit upon the correct solution."

"I think you ought to acknowledge your success," I said.

Holmes rapped on the cabman's panel. "Driver, turn around. Take another route," he said.

He folded his arms again and refused to be drawn into further discussion until, after what seemed hours but was really more like forty more minutes, we finally reached home and mounted the steps to our sitting room.

I had earlier given up the hope of a cold drink and a relaxing hour on our sofa, followed by a leisurely supper at one of our favourite restaurants. After hearing Holmes's regrets about his previous delay, I expected him to take immediate action.

But when Holmes opened our hallway door, I realized our path would have to go in a different direction.

Mycroft Holmes awaited us.

About the Authors

Anna Elliott is the author of the *Twilight of Avalon* trilogy, and *The Pride and Prejudice Chronicles*. She was delighted to lend a hand in giving the character of Lucy James her own voice, firstly because she loves Sherlock Holmes as much as her father, Charles Veley, and second because it almost never happens that someone with a dilemma shouts, "Quick, we need an author of historical fiction!" She lives in Pennsylvania with her husband and four children.

Charles Veley is the author of the first two books in this series of fresh Sherlock Holmes adventures. He is thrilled to be contributing Dr. Watson's chapters for the series, and delighted beyond words to be collaborating with Anna Elliott.

Printed in Great Britain
by Amazon